D1422061

A BREEZE OF MORNING

A BREEZE
OF MORNING

BY

CHARLES MORGAN

For a breeze of morning moves,
And the planet of Love is on high . . .
TENNYSON

Jorge Pinto Books Inc.
New York

A Breeze of Morning

Jorge Pinto Books Inc. by arrangement with the Estate of Charles Morgan through Scott Ferris Associates, UK. All rights reserved. Jorge Pinto Books Inc. 151 East 58th Street, New York, New York, 10022.

Book preparation services by Charles King, website: www.ckmm.com

Cover design: Susan Hildebrand

This edition of *A Breeze of Morning* is published under the Rediscovered Books series of Jorge Pinto Books Inc.

ISBN: 1-934978-06-X
978-1-934978-06-1

TO HENRY

HIS FATHER-IN-LAW DEDICATES THIS BOOK

ACKNOWLEDGEMENTS

THE poet Gray has fortunately provided an English version of the four lines of Latin which appear on page 197. Readers whose Latinity, like my own, is small and far away, are asked neither to give me credit for these Elegiacs nor to think that the boy in my story, to whom they are attributed, must have been impossibly precocious. They were written for me by a young Etonian, Mr. S. H. Willink, K.S., whose kindness I gratefully acknowledge.

I offer my thanks also to Mr. Daniel Macmillan, Mr. C. R. N. Routh, Mr. C. H. Taylor and Mr. B. C. Whitfield for the help they have given me. If error remain, it arises from my own failure to make good use of their counsel.

C. M.

CONTENTS

PART ONE

THE MASK AND THE FACE

1

A MONTH ago, before the event occurred which has led me to attempt this account of the past, my sister and I spoke one evening of Rose Letterby and what became of her. It was a rare subject between us. I recall it for that reason and because Ann's view of my share in the matter surprised me.

I told her more than she already knew, though perhaps not much more than she had guessed, of my boyhood's part in the tale. As it had all happened so long ago, it was easy for us both to smile at the absurdities of my behaviour — easier than to speak too seriously of memories that touched wounds in us both; and I was still smiling at my own expense when I said : " What you don't grasp, Ann, is——"

" Oh yes I do," she interrupted quietly. " You loved her yourself in your own way. Anyhow, you were enchanted. Young though you were, it isn't as exceptional as you think."

My feeling of surprise when she said this may be evidence of my having become stiff-minded. As we grow older, we begin to take conventional views of childhood, and the conventions change like the fashions. Once it was fashionable to pretend that all children were whimsical creatures who knew no difference between kisses and thimbles ; more recently that they were a tribe of savages. We adopt these conventions — of which the most misleading is that

" boys will be boys " — because it is easier to laugh at our young visions and to pack away our follies into convenient boxes than to remember how much we saw and how many different kinds of thing at the same time. We are wise to hesitate a little before exclaiming : " No schoolboy would ever notice *that*! No schoolgirl would ever feel it ! " Shakespeare's Juliet was a child by our reckoning.

It may even be true — and the thought encourages me to write what I have to write — that a boy's view of the love of others older than himself has value, in spite of its inexperience, simply because it is not jaded.

I confess that I am now conventional enough to explain the depth and intensity of my feeling in those far-off days by recalling that, in some respects, I was, at the end of my fourteenth year, uncommonly mature. I had spent more of my thought on the classics and Shakespeare than was usual at my age, even in the early years of the century. But this explanation may be uncalled for. It is always a temptation to suppose oneself a rarity. Perhaps Ann was right, and the sense I had then of looking through the masks that people wear, and even, now and again, of putting off my own — that is to say, of being inside the legend for a time — is common enough. Certainly the experience, when it comes, does not last long ; ordinary life goes on after it ; ordinary life goes on during it. It strikes me as mysterious and significant that, in our moments of vision, the mask and the face should often be visible at the same time — even Rose Letterby's, even my own : and that when, for a little while, one is inside the room of another's life, one is still, so ridiculously, a face at the window.

4

2

THE evening which singles itself out as a point of departure must have been towards the end of an Easter term. Across a gulf of more than forty years, only feeling lives, and even the feeling of that hour, as I came away from school between daylight and dusk, may be tempered in recollection by the knowledge which I have now of what was to happen to me before I reached home and of what should I find when I came there. Certainly the moment presents itself to my mind as having been in some way luminous, like an incoming wave that lifts up its green, transparent crest into the light before it curls over, breaks and is dissipated in froth.

It was later than usual. On certain days of each week, four of us, who were to try for Eton scholarships that summer, went to Mr. Libbett, the headmaster, for special coaching when ordinary school was done. Two of the four, Tony Seaford and I, were day-boys, and we came away together. We had known each other all our lives, had built houses in trees together, constructed elaborate railway systems with clock-work trains, and even shared a visiting governess before our promotion to Libbett's preparatory school. He was naturally gay and light-hearted, having none of my feeling that to be a boy was to wear a tiresome disguise which I was impatient to outgrow. I had often done his work for him and he had taught me games — a distribution of labour which suited us well, for neither of us was a muff in the other's world; he could take in the rules of Latin verse if they were repeated often enough with diagrams and jingles to aid his memory, and though nothing would ever make my hand and eye and body move together as his did in the spontaneous harmony of an athlete, I could learn pretty well what to do with my feet and how to hold a racquet or a bat. I tried hard to be good at games and moderately succeeded; he inherited a kingdom.

That he would win a scholarship, no one had the least hope. It was, he had told us with his wide, easy smile, not his father's but his mother's idea that he should join the Scholarship Class, and Mr. Libbett, I suppose, admitted him to it because he could deny nothing to a boy so clearly destined to play games for Eton, Cambridge and England. Tony, whose whole family tradition was athletic, took an extremely offhand view of my gnawing anxiety about my scholarship, while a failure to obtain it appeared to me as a failure in life itself. My father, perhaps unconsciously, had taught me by his hard work, his freedom from self-indulgence and his unswerving advance in his own profession as an engineer, to see the future as a huge ladder to be climbed step by step. To miss a rung was to be lost — perhaps to fall back for ever into the company of those he called " the ne'er-do-weels ", and this evening, as a consequence of a view Mr. Libbett had taken of my Latin prose, this pit was yawning at my feet.

" I shan't get it, you know," I said, expecting to be contradicted, but Tony answered casually: " Good

6

Lord, why not? . . . And even if you don't—" He took a squash-ball out of his pocket and began to juggle with it over the back of his hand and his wrist in a way that made it seem attached to him by invisible elastic. " Can you do that? " He took another ball from his pocket and gave it me. " Try."

I took the ball, clutched it, and after a little while handed it back.

At the end of the school drive, we turned down a long, muddy lane known as the Private Road. On one side of it, over the hedge, were the empty playing-fields and beyond them on higher ground the school-buildings, from which, as we moved, spikes of bare gaslight flashed and vanished through a belt of monkey-puzzle. On the other side was a high, steep, grassy bank, and beyond the bank a rising wood that threw up a serrated edge against the sky. Tony sprang up the bank in three strides taken at an angle as though he were performing a triple high-jump, and with a friendly shout to me, disappeared over a stile into the wood. This was his shortest way home.

My own took me past the little branch-line railway station from which my father made his hour's journey to London every morning. Upon it the roads of Letterby, running down between ridges, converged like the grooves of a scallop-shell. Beyond the railway station and with my back to it, I began to climb the road, called Farthing Hill, which would take me home. School being left behind me for the long night, I returned, as I always did on this stretch of road when I passed along it alone, into that condition of feeling time and place within me like tremors of the blood rather than of seeing them with a naturalist's objective eye, which was my way of being released from my disguises. In that mood, as it opened and opened, anything was possible: that the homing rooks should leave silver lines engraved upon the air, that the bead of afternoon rain still clinging to the thorn-leaf should slide and fall as I counted seven, or that Mr. Crutwell, who was walking ahead of me in the top-hat he wore in the City and with an umbrella crooked on his black sleeve, should turn out when I overtook him not to have Mr. Crutwell's face. In view of that awkward possibility, I was careful not to overtake him, and loitered in the hedgerow until he had gone up his own side-turning to the left. Then I moved on again, thinking cheerfully that my sister, having kept late tea for me, would be in the morning-room now with early lamplight on the coloured silk in her needle and on her lap; and feeling at the same time, with a shudder of delight, that the spring air was dividing to let my face pass through it, and would close behind me when I was gone, like the sea in the wake of a ship. So I began to run uphill to make the bow-wave rise about my temples, and stopped in wonder because I had suddenly remembered that Mr. Crutwell's wife had been buried a week ago.

There was no one, except, of course, servants, in the house to which he was returning, and it became for me wildly possible that there would be no one in mine. The bright silks would be in their basket, wood-ashes in the grate. If Ann were dead, the blinds would be down, and still, though she were dead, I must do my home-work, for no evening must be wasted, no rung in the ladder missed. This imagining halted me. I turned and looked down Farthing Hill, knowing that my sister was not dead, neither deluded nor frightened, but with the ache of Mr. Crutwell's solitude within me, as though I too were old ; and so I must have stood a little while, with an awe of miracles shining down upon me from the elm-crests and the gold-plunging rooks, because my sister had been dead and was alive again, and I had been old and was young.

When I began to climb again, anxiety for my scholarship returned to me, but for a little while I had slipped out of the skin of being a schoolboy : that disguise which I had still to wear for so many years to come and which no one except Ann had eyes to penetrate.

Where Farthing Hill flattened out, the open gates of Letterby Manor appeared on my right. They had always stood open as long as I could remember ; their hinges — for I had tried them once when no one was looking — were clogged by rust ; and over one of them ivy had entwined itself in the wrought iron, choking the heraldic lion of Mr. Letterby's crest, and throwing its tendrils up the brick gate-pillar to a mouldering stone ball at the summit. On the farther side of the gates, in a tiny fenced garden of its own, was a cottage or lodge which an old gardener of Mr. Letterby's was understood to inhabit, but the fence was a gaping entanglement of weeds and splinters, the windows were blinded by great eyebrows of creeper, and the little wooden gate stood always in the same position, neither open nor shut, its grey slats bulging outward like a donkey's broken knees.

My road at this point followed a wide curve round Letterby Park. It would lead, after a plain dull mile, to my father's house, the garden of which had been carved out of the park and was separated from it now only by a woody dingle. Beyond my home, over the hill-brow, the road fell gently to what we called " the river ", a shallow but pleasant stream with the proud name of Little Thames. On its banks stood the village of Slipton, which, having no railway station nearer than ours, clung to old-fashioned rural prides and held itself aloof from our " suburbanism ". Across Letterby Park there was a public footpath leading into the main road at the outskirts of Slipton, and an earlier branch from this footpath would take me, beside the dingle, almost to my own gate. It was a short-cut which my family seldom used, for Mr. Letterby was believed deeply to resent the passing of strangers through his grounds, though they had an ancient right over this path, and my father, who regarded him as " an awkward neighbour ", was determined not to be " beholden to him ". My father himself took the longer route to the station every day, as I knew well, for I accompanied him on my way to school. Once, when his infallible watch had misled him, we had plunged through the dingle and emerged, with a sense of adventure that had made my father laugh at himself, by the mossy drive and the wrought-iron gates. On other rare occasions in the remote past I had persuaded unwarned nursemaids to risk Tom Tiddler's ground. But " The Right of Way ", though used often enough by the Slipton folk, was now generally abstained from by us — largely, I think, because Mr. Letterby was spoken of as one who " thought he still owned the parish as his ancestors had done " and who regarded all professional or business men as intruders. It was in my father's pride not to " creep past under the old

ogre's windows ", and perhaps it was in his con-
servatism as well, for, though he would joke about " the
Squire " privately, he allowed no one to speak of him
with disrespect. " A proud old fossil " was the hardest
phrase I ever heard him use of Mr. Letterby.

3

THIS evening, as usual, I started out along the high road, having twisted the satchel containing my school-books into a more comfortable position on my back. My right hand found unexpectedly in a side-pocket what felt like a postcard. On examination it turned out to be a chess-problem which, as Ann and I had failed to solve it on the previous evening, I had cut out from the newspaper and pasted on the card for later attack.

Ann had not shown as much interest in this problem as she ordinarily did in those we tackled together. She had been talking to my father about my cousin Howard who was coming to live with us because he was poor and his parents' death had left him with nowhere else to live while he made his way as a barrister. " Oh, you make no doubt," my father had said, " with his brains and application there'll be no stopping Howard."

The recollection of this praise of my father's, reflected in Ann's attentive face, brought me to a standstill. What would I not have given to be the occasion of it ! But would it not surprise her, I thought, if I were to solve the chess-problem without her help ? So much of what was pleasing in life consisted in its being shared with my sister or being brought to her as an offering, an achievement, that I pressed my whole mind, all my skill, my memory, my inventiveness, under those rooky trees on the fringe of Letterby Park, into discovering how White should move and mate in three moves. From which intense preoccupation — for I had put the card back into my pocket and was carrying the chess-board in my mind — my mind slid away, as the mind will from an over-charge, and, looking round me, I thought: What would have happened if, instead of coming by the high road, I had turned in at the wrought-iron gates? Where should I have been now? On the slimy gravel under the deep vaulting of the avenue. . . . And if, instead of branching off from the drive into the Right of Way, I had gone on to the house itself, and knocked, and knocked, and pealed the bell, someone would have come. Then, what should I have said? Nothing. But something, I told myself, would have happened that won't happen now, that will never happen if I go on by the high road, and I saw the not-happening as a shining bubble of time lifted away from me into the air.

Back then. Through the open gates. But in fairy stories the three wishes are granted always in a variant of the wisher's design, and I did not go to the door and knock. Instead, turning soon leftward, I followed dutifully the Right of Way, looking always to my right — without seeming to look — at the long, melancholy façade of the Manor. There was ground-mist now in the close meadows; the house itself, mounted on its invisible garden beyond the ha-ha, seemed to be afloat, and the crests of its near trees to be trunkless and rising. It was as though the house's dimmed whiteness were about to dissolve in the pearly air. Only its windows — nine on the floor above the portico,

four on either side of it, each of twelve panes — were
hard and opaque. Leaning on an iron gate, I watched
the yawning fixity of their gleam. On the leftward
edge of each pane at that moment the sun engraved
itself with a fiery needle, and the walls shone. A little
cascade of music, so faint that I saw rather than heard
it, rippled in the light, and was gone when the walls
dulled and the windows blackened. There could have
been no music to hear. The house was too far away.
It was as if crystal and crystal had touched in the
dividing air.

" What is it you are looking at ? "

I stared round into the Squire's face, not far above
me, for I was tall for my age.

" The Manor, sir."

" No — in your hand."

The postcard, surprisingly, had come out of my
pocket and was in my right hand. With the other I
grabbed my cap off.

" Let me look. . . . Cover yourself, pray."

After a moment's doubt, I understood this to mean
that I should put on my cap.

" Well, I take it the first move is the pawn's, eh ? "

" We tried that, sir. It leaves him free to castle.
Then he's away."

" Ah . . . Well . . . Don't it work ? Maybe not."
Then he looked up from the postcard. " Who's ' we,'
by the by ? "

" My sister and I."

" And where do you come from ? "

I pointed homeward.

" What, Harbrook the churchwarden's son from
over the dingle ? I thought he was quite a little boy."

I scarcely recognized my father, one of the leading railway engineers in England, as "Harbrook the churchwarden", but the rest of the speech pleased me well enough. Mr. Letterby at close quarters was astonishingly different from the legendary figure which stalked in and out of church but was not otherwise seen: different, chiefly, because what had always before been thought of as an effigy was now visibly breathing and had long, ribbed hands with streaks of grey hair between knuckle and finger-joint. That he should be thrusting his lower lip out over my chess-problem was exceedingly odd; his ancestor on the Letterby tomb might as probably have come out of his stone armour and walked and talked. His face was ruddier and more leathery than I had supposed it to be. Under his prominent cheek-bones were little pits which deepened when he thrust his lip out and gave a liveliness to what had always before seemed a masklike and impersonal severity.

"This wants setting on a board," he said. "My day's past for doing these things on paper."

Some reply seemed to be expected of me, for his eyes looked inquiringly into mine. As I said nothing, he threw up his head as though the flight of a bird had caught his attention, and, gazing skyward, began to slide my postcard into his pocket.

"You won't mind, I take it, if I borrow this?" and if I had not spoken at once he would have been gone.

"But, *sir*——" I began.

"You do mind? Well, bless my soul, it's your property," but he made no move of surrender.

"You see, it's my sister's too."

" Ah," he said, " awkward." Then after consideration he added with slow reluctance : " There's only one thing for it. You'd better come up to the Manor while I set my chess-table. Then you can have the card."

We set out on a silent trudge. Presumably, he forgot my existence, for when I had followed him through a side-door into a narrow lobby full of mackintoshes and walking-sticks, he rediscovered me in the half-darkness.

" Ah . . . Oh yes. Come in."

4

THE room we entered had three long windows from the garden but they threw a pallor rather than a light on to a central table, piled with books and papers and biscuit-tins, and on to a wall of bookshelves reaching to the ceiling. The fire seemed to be out, but when Mr. Letterby threw four or five logs on to the ashes they began to smoulder. Telling me to " be seated ", he set about lighting a lamp.

The chair I found was a soft, shabby continent of leather, long ago turned to the colour of a reddish sand. I sat in its north-west corner, put my satchel beside me to the east, and watched the match-light on my host's left ear and the window-light on his stooping back, in which the vertebrae appeared. Music came down to me again, a snatch of it, then a silence, then another snatch; it was as though a kitten were playing lazily with a tinkling ball. The sound was almost as thin as it had been when I was in the park, and I thought of it as coming from a solitary tower. There was no tower in the Manor, but the words " solitary tower " spoke themselves in my mind, and, as I had been reading about Josephine, I saw in the tower, standing at her piano, and walking away from it, and returning to let her fingers idle over the keys, a lady, presumably a princess, in the straight, white, high-waisted dress of the First Empire. Her face did not appear, but, like all princesses, she was more beautiful than a new moon.

" M' daughter," Mr. Letterby said. " Since she came back she's always tinkling. Can't keep her door or windows shut. Like her poor mother in that."

Between us on the hearth was a square stool, perhaps eighteen inches high, covered by a fringed cloth. On the cloth were a used tea-cup, a biscuit-tin, pipes, papers, books, an open tobacco-jar, a slipper with pencils stuck in it, and a bronze lion — part of the general débris that spread over the room like a pall of cobwebs. Everything appeared to have remained where it had happened to be put down at the beginning of time. Books lay open dustily as though they had long ago tired of waiting for some dead reader to continue his reading.

Mr. Letterby put the used tea-cup on to the nearest resting-place, which happened to be the stone kerb of the hearth, and reached out his hand towards the slipper. Observing that he intended to clear the stool, I moved forward to help, though I could see no vacant space into which the lion and all else could be put. The same difficulty found him untroubled. He picked up the cloth by its corners and put it, with all it contained, on to the floor. The biscuit-tin and the lion rattled together, the slipper gave up its cargo of pencils, the papers crinkled and were silent. In many parts of the floor were corresponding dumps which now explained themselves.

The naked stool was revealed as an inlaid chess-table. It contained a drawer where chessmen reposed in slots of green baize. Those that the problem called for were taken out and set in their places with a murmur of reference to the diagram. Never had I seen such pieces. The red castle must have been all of five inches high with its carved flag.

When the arrangement was complete and I supposed that we were to attack the problem together, my postcard was unexpectedly handed back to me, and I grasped that my presence was no longer required. Still, as no word of dismissal had been spoken, I was shy of going. Moving in my chair, I reached for my satchel, but so clumsily that it fell and books were tipped out of it. One, my Virgil, slid to Mr. Letterby's feet. He picked it up, opened it at hazard, held it to the lamp, and, seeming to forget our chess-problem, curled himself sideways in his chair and began to read. This paralysed me. Having the postcard in my pocket, I was free to creep out of the room as far as that was concerned; but he had my Virgil and I couldn't do my homework without it. I sat waiting and staring. Music came down from the tower, recognizably a mazurka that Ann played sometimes, but it tailed away at the first difficulty and stopped.

Mr. Letterby had ceased to read and was watching me.

" Whose markings are these ? "

" Mine," I said.

" Your own or the schoolmaster's ? "

I admitted that some were difficult passages that Mr. Libbett had told us were likely to be " given ".

Coming to life as I had not seen him do before, Mr. Letterby tapped the page. " For example, this passage :

> *Dixit, et avertens rosea cervice refulsit,*
> *ambrosiaeque comae divinum vertice odorem*
> *spiravere. . . .*

Do you remember? The goddess Venus has appeared to Aeneas in the guise of a huntress, and he has felt the divine quality in her — *namque haud tibi voltus mortalis*, but he hasn't guessed who she is. And then, when she was turning away, *avertens*, her neck shone 'rose-flushed' and — can you go on?"

" ' And her ambrosial hair,' " I began, " —' and the immortal tresses on her head breathed celestial——' "

" ' Hair ' will do. Leave out *ambrosiae* for the moment; it means two things at once — the fragrance and the immortality. Go on, if you can."

But Mr. Letterby had the text; I was remembering. " ' And her hair,' " I began again, " ' breathed . . . breathed out the scent of heaven ' — or something like that, sir, isn't it?"

"Something very like that," he answered with a sigh. "Now, tell me, why did you mark that? Why is it likely to be ' given ' ? Anyhow: ' given ' in what, may I ask?"

"In my scholarship exam." And encouraged first by his questions, then by his attention, I told him my trouble and my fears. I told him even of Mr. Libbett's quarrel with my prose. "You see, sir," I explained, " he's frightfully hot on Cicero. He always says: ' Cicero wouldn't have written that,' and I can't say back to him ' But Tacitus might have.' Even if I did, he'd only say: ' You play safe. You stick to Cicero. Then as far as the Examiners are concerned you can't go wrong.' He always says that. And then he says: ' It's just a question, Harbrook, whether you want to get that scholarship or whether you want to show off.' "

"And which do you want?" Mr. Letterby inquired with a shrewd glance; but before I could reply he was tapping the book again: " Listen: *Dixit, et avertens rosea cervice refulsit,*" and he read aloud to the point at which the goddess, rising in the air, departs for Paphos.

To hear Virgil read as poetry, straight on like a ship under sail, and not dissected, was new to me. It gave me precisely what Mr. Libbett could not, or would not, give.

" You have marked that passage in pencil, not in ink as you have most of them. Is that one of your schoolmaster's markings? "

" No, sir."

" Did you mark it at school at all? "

" N-no, sir."

" Where then? "

I swallowed, and looked at the chess-board, and answered that I had marked it in bed.

" These in pencil," he said, turning the pages. " All marked in bed? Why did you mark them? Not, surely, because they were specially difficult? "

" Because I liked them," I answered.

He shut the book and handed it back. " That's what I wanted to know. Our tastes accord." Standing up, he added: " I might be of use to you. Who teaches you when Libbett don't? "

I then asked him a question which has never ceased to astonish my recollection. Perhaps the adjective came to me out of the mazurka, which had begun again overhead. I asked: " Are you a secret scholar? "

His laugh was like the single bark of a surprised dog. " Yes," he said and cocked up his head as he had in the open air when pocketing my chess-problem. " Whether I can teach you is another question. Teaching is a technical job like training a horse, anyhow *coaching* is, and I, as you observe " — he gave a twist to his mouth at once wry and humorous — " am not systematic. Still, you could learn from me, I make no doubt. Or we could play chess. Come again, if you like. Have a biscuit."

Glad to be given something to do, I took a biscuit out of the tin and began to munch it while I strapped my satchel. Because I was no longer thinking of myself as a schoolboy or of him in his conventional disguise of " The Squire ", I began to put to him another problem of mine. The *rules* of Latin verse were one thing, I could follow them; but the sound was another, and I couldn't for the life of me *hear* what difference it made when certain rules were broken. For example, if you said: *Tempora mutantur nos et mutamur in illis*, that was full marks, but if you said *et nos* it was a crime. I couldn't see what difference it made to —

" To a Roman ear ? "

" Well, yes."

" That, you see," Mr. Letterby said, " is why you could learn from me." And he continued after a long pause, quietly and calmly: " I was a Roman once. Of that I'm pretty sure."

To this remark there seemed to be no appropriate answer. Mr. Letterby settled down again beside the chess-table. I let myself out of the house and walked home.

5

I**T** was my custom on arriving there to walk round the corner of the house to the morning-room and there knock on the window to let Ann know I was come. She was always there at that hour, not with household sewing as she might be in dutiful periods of the day, but with embroidery or *gros point* which were her art and pleasure. At my knock she would raise her head with eager recognition, come to the door and let me in. Though she was my elder by several years and had run the house since my mother's death, we did not count the years, particularly at that time of the evening, which was for both of us an end of the day's outward travelling; we talked together of what interested us. Or so it seemed to me, though perhaps it was I who talked and she who listened. Certainly this interlude in the day was important to me — a coming into harbour for fresh stores and water.

This evening, because I was so late, the plane of window-light had the sharpness of winter's definition. The upper surfaces of laurel beneath the sill had a steely shine; the pathway gravel was like glass beads; and yet, beyond the path, where the light flattened out on the grassy verge, white and yellow crocuses leapt like flames. A wave of happiness or, rather, of intense peacefulness ran through me. I was no longer afraid of life — not even of my scholarship — but felt myself adventurously included in it. How much I had to tell Ann of the Manor and the Old Roman! How she would listen! I felt as though I had come home from a long voyage, full of bronze lions and mazurkas. Nothing was dreary or impossible. I looked forward to everything.

But when I had pressed my way through the bushes and looked into the window, none of the evening ritual fulfilled itself. Howard had arrived. He was standing with his back to me. A well-trimmed head, a white collar, a neat black jacket and striped trousers with an iron crease, were all that I saw at first, and even when these moved and Howard's keen profile appeared I found that Ann was not in her accustomed chair but in the high one she chose sometimes to receive visitors. Her hands were clasping and unclasping themselves in her lap, her eyes followed his movement, and when she in her turn began to speak it was with an uptilting of her head, a kind of dancing animation, that I did not recognize. He leaned forward, his hands behind his back, laughed, said something; she responded — I couldn't hear her laughter though I had heard his, but her teeth gleamed, her eyes shone. Their lips moved, they were talking together, talking each other down — how eagerly! I had not guessed before that my sister was so young.

To have knocked on the window now would have been meaningless. I slid back through the laurels and heard the nails in my school-boots crunch into the gravel. It was my custom to take my boots off in the hall and go, stockinged, into the morning-room where my red slippers would be, but I thought it best, as there was a visitor, not to go into the morning-room until I had washed, and brushed my hair; there were other slippers in my bedroom. So I walked round the house through the earthy night-smells, let myself in by the side-door, went to my bedroom, turned up the gas, let my satchel slide down from my shoulder, and sat on my bed.

Having taken off my boots, I went to the cupboard for my old black slippers, wondering if they were respectable enough to wear at dinner, and found the red ones still there. It was natural enough that she should have forgotten them this evening in showing Howard his room and settling him in. Suddenly I was glad that he had come. It was exciting. Not that I knew him as she did, for she had stayed at his house when his mother was alive, but I had known him during his return visits, and last summer he had shared our seaside holiday. I had found that he always " stretched " me in the way I liked, and gave me confidence by having such unswerving confidence in himself. I remembered going into his room at night and doing exercises with him and afterwards sitting on the foot of his bed to talk.

He learned from me also. There were things I knew more about than he did: railways, for example, of which I had learned from my father, and Shakespeare. He made me talk about them, understood what I was trying to say almost before I had said it, was never bored, never forgot. It was all grist to his mill. " One can't go about the world *not* knowing Shakespeare. People refer to him. I can't think why I have been vague about him so long," and that summer, when we had bathed and everyone else was lying about sleepily, he would go off by himself and read Shakespeare for ninety minutes by his watch. I asked how much he had read. The speed was gigantic. At night he would say: " Well, if you don't believe it, cross-examine me." I myself knew less than he gave me credit for, but I questioned him from the book. He never failed on story or character ; again and again, if I gave him a line, he could go on. . . . Oh yes, you can say he read Shakespeare as if he were reading a brief. So he did, but that was his disguise. He was enraptured too. There are minds capable of that.

I had been spellbound by his prowess, by what I can recognize now as an advocate's power to differentiate and call into use unconfusedly all the energies of his impersonal mind, and at the same time I was drawn to him by the ease, the warmth, the insatiable interest of his personal relationships. A room could freeze when he was in it, but it could glow too, as the morning-room had so evidently been glowing when I looked into it. I had felt excluded then. Now in my red slippers I caught the glow and began to look forward to the evening. First, I would do my hair and wash, then settle down to work for ninety minutes, as he would have done. In that way, by unremitting-ness, by not standing and staring at irrelevant princesses or solitary towers, the ladder was to be climbed.

With a determined step I went to the mirror. The head I saw there was still wearing its school-cap — pink, with a grey peak. I wish I had thrown it down and trampled on it, but that, though the impulse came, seemed in itself a childishness. I took it off, hitched it to the brass knob of the bedstead and unstrapped my satchel.

6

Howard Treladdin had long been a favourite subject of my father's. Scholarship after scholarship. Firsts at Cambridge. Firsts in his Bar Exams. " Not that that in itself means anything at the Bar," my father conceded, " but you watch him . . . ."

He was the son of my father's favourite sister, " the cleverest of the girls ", who had been thrown away on Harry Treladdin " with his piano and his songs ".

Ann had said once that she liked Uncle Harry when she was a little girl. " Of course you did, my dear," my father had answered. " You're a woman too. They all did. Too many of them. Not that there was anything against your Uncle Harry, you understand, except that he was Irish and couldn't keep a sixpence in his pocket. And Howard certainly doesn't take after his father in that respect, though he does strum the piano."

In my father's view, piano-playing was a feminine accomplishment, but Howard had strengths which were more than compensation for this romantic weakness. He made a little money go a very long way. He took care of his clothes and always " looked as if he kept a valet ". He had an ambition like steel and didn't know what it was to spare himself. " Make no mistake," my father said. " Give him half a dozen years at the Bar and he'll be well up the ladder."

Howard's coming to live with us disturbed the routine of our household less than I had expected. He went to chambers by an earlier train than my father's, so that my morning walks on my way to school remained as they had been. In the company of others my father always parentally remembered my age, but to be alone with him was a kind of promotion; he treated me then as a companion, and these walks were precious to me.

Contrary to my first intention, I had told no one of my visit to the Manor. No opportunity had arisen on the evening of Howard's arrival, our conversation having centred in him, and by the next day the library and the " tower " and the mazurka had become for me a private adventure that I didn't want to talk about. Even when one evening Howard and Ann were at the piano together, experimenting in duets, and she, in an interval, played the mazurka's opening bars, I held fast to my secret. It became deeper and more legendary. Mr. Letterby had said: " Come again, if you like," and I often recalled his words. I shall go some day, I said to myself, but as I might have said, after reading *The Arabian Nights*: some day I shall go to Baghdad.

Nevertheless one morning as I set out with my father I said to him: " Let's go across the park."

" Oh no," he said.

" But it is a Right of Way, isn't it ? "

" Oh yes, it's a Right of Way."

But we went by the longer route.

" You know, David," he said, " when I think of all we have to be thankful for — work, a full life, opportunity everywhere — I feel sorry for that old man. It's

28

true, he has brought it on himself, clinging to a place he can't afford to keep up. Still . . ."

" But isn't he rich ? He must be."

" I dare say he's well off on paper."

" What does that mean — ' on paper ' ? "

" Only that he has no money free. Nothing to spend. Not the price of a lick of paint. Mortgaged up to the hilt."

My father explained. The Letterby family had been rich enough once. Then they *had* owned the whole parish and much more. In the eighteenth century they had gambled it away, so it was said, and since then things had gone from bad to worse.

" And then, Mrs. Letterby was no good," my father continued. " One of those flighty Continental women. Always in the newspapers in a huge picture-hat. ' The Beautiful Mrs. Letterby ' . . . oh, she was a beauty I grant you, a very famous beauty, and generous when it suited her, so they say. Generous with her husband's money, and extravagant as the day is long."

Then my father's old-fashion asserted itself. " No tradition to keep her on the rails. Her father, before he became a lord and called himself Comberagh, was chiefly boots and shoes. The best of him was his joke against himself : that anyhow he had ' climbed on his own feet '. . . . Of course, Mrs. Letterby and the Squire didn't get on, but that's no excuse for her being always away. Fluttering home for a week when it suited her and sweeping into the Manor-pew for all the world as if it were a box at a theatre. Then away again. With her daughter, too. Spending and spending. Cannes. Nice. Monte Carlo. No good. And then, of course, what happens ? Her brother, the present Lord

Comberagh, steps in to the rescue, and he no better than herself. The old story of mortgagor and mortgagee."

I inquired who were this mysterious couple, Morgy Jaw and Morgy Gee, and my father, to whom debt was a sin, improved the occasion.

" Well," he said, " it's like this, David, and let it be a warning to you. You know your Shakespeare better than I do by a long chalk. Didn't he say : ' Neither a borrower nor a lender be ' ? "

" Polonius did, in *Hamlet*."

" Quite right too. Couldn't be better advice for a youngster setting out in life. If a friend wants to borrow fifty, far better to give him five ; then he won't come again."

But I wanted the story and inquired how this Lord — Lord what's-his-name—came into it ?

" Now you're asking," my father replied. " Of course, I have none of the detail. It's only by some chance talk in the City that I happen to know that Lord Comberagh is mortgagee. And the jumped-up kind give nothing for nothing. I suppose what happened is roughly that Mrs. L. ran up debts galli- vanting in Europe. The Squire had to pay up and he hadn't the money. So he borrowed it from her brother on the security of the estate ; and her brother, being a rascal and knowing just how he was placed, took a stiffish rate of interest. I don't know, but that's how I figure it out. . . . And now, what with taxation going up and up, when the Squire has paid his interest — if he can pay even that — he has nothing left. And if he doesn't pay, the mortgagee has him."

" In what way ' has him ' ? "

" Sells him up. Turns him out of the house. Mrs.

Letterby's death may mend matters a bit. That stops the leak, you might say. But there's still the daughter. And in any case the wife's death may cut both ways. She was the mortgagee's sister; that may have made him hold his hand while she lived. Now, he'll be after his money."

My private visit to Mr. Letterby had given me an active sympathy with him. After all, it was not he who had run into debt; to turn him out of his house for no fault of his own, was gross injustice. Scoundrels and the young, for different reasons, are always against a lender, once his money is lent.

As I walked at my father's side and drew in the spring air, which was sweet that morning after a night of showers, I was afflicted not so much by the cruelty as by the inexplicable unreason of a world in which such monsters as Morgy Gee could exist or wish to exist. It had always surprised me, when I had read fairy tales or *Paradise Lost*, that anyone was ever found to play the villain's part. Why did Satan rebel? He must have known that he would lose in the end. Why did Shylock so persistently put himself in the wrong, when it was quite obvious that he hadn't a chance? Why, if it came to that, should the Wicked Fairy plan and plan to make the Princess prick her finger, when it must have been clear that the Princess would not die but fall asleep and, in the end, awake?

These were questions upon which my father was unlikely to have a helpful opinion, but I asked him what Mr. Letterby's daughter was like.

" Bless my soul, you must have seen her in church with her mother once or twice. Don't you remember a girl with hair right down to her waist? We called

her ' Harvest Festival ' — she was so spick and span
and her hair the colour of wheat."

" Oh yes," I answered, surprised by the recollection,
" but I mean, what is she like now ? "

" I haven't seen her except at her mother's funeral,"
my father replied, " and once since then, waiting for a
train at Charing Cross. I believe Hugh and Marjorie
Seaford have dealings with her, but she doesn't appear
much locally. Doesn't even come to church on
Sunday mornings."

My father's disapproval silenced me. The subject
seemed likely to drop, when, having cut down a road-
side thistle with his walking-stick, he unexpectedly continued : " It seems a pity for a young girl if this is to
be her home. She can't be much above eighteen.
You'd have thought she'd have been glad of young
company — Ann's, for example. But it's her business,
I suppose. Probably she has her own set outside —
Continental johnnies, no doubt. If she's like her
mother, we aren't smart enough for her."

" Is she like her mother ? "

" You'll often find, David, that character——"

" To look at, I mean. When you *saw* her on the
platform at Charing Cross ? "

My father considered this for a moment and
answered in a less severe voice : " Oh well, beauty is
but skin deep."

There was time enough before I was due at school.
When my father had gone into the railway station, I
went slowly on my way up the Private Road, loitering
in the hedges for their scent and sparkle and for the
faces to be discovered in them under dewy crowns.
And what on earth will happen to *her*, I wondered, if

32

Morgy Gee turns Mr. Letterby out of doors? I saw her as a fugitive, running down the avenue towards the wrought-iron gates. The avenue was a tunnel whose roof closed in upon her; her long hair streamed behind her on the night wind; the ivy stretched out its tentacles to arrest her, but she passed through them unscathed and the darkness flowed away from her, rebuked. Her face did not appear, only the sparkle of her racing eyes, bright as the spring's diadem.

The door by which I entered the school led into a passage where gym shoes were kept in numbered pigeon-holes. Full of boys' shouting and the screech of nailed boots on tiles, it smelt of rubber and dust.

7

Our household was enlivened by Howard's presence in it. He made us all talk and laugh, and introduced variety into our affairs. I went with him to the Boat Race, watching it from a place of privilege in the house of one of his friends, where he appeared to know everyone and behaved with a gay self-confidence that dazzled me. He took Ann to a play. She dressed at home, he in chambers; they dined at a restaurant and, after the theatre, returned by the last train. This in itself was revolutionary, for my father held that to come home at one in the morning and carry a bag up the hill was a game not worth the candle; our rare playgoing was confined to *matinées* and my father himself would not dine in London if he could by any means avoid it. But Howard's frequently late hours were approved because, whether they were or were not a pleasure also, they were certainly a professional exercise. " A young barrister making his way must dine out for his living. I know only too well that I have neglected the social side of life too much. It's just a question of stamina."

Howard had stamina enough. No doubt he spent in London, with a sufficiently lavish air, what he was bound to spend, and towards those he loved he could be generous, too; but as soon as he was, so to speak, out of sight, he spent nothing on himself. No porters;

he carried his own bag. No hired cab from the livery stables, even to meet the last train. However often he came home late, he set out at the same hour in the morning, and I have known him again and again, after a late return, work at his briefs.

The room given to him adjoined my own, which had, perhaps, once been its dressing-room. There was a communicating door. I think it was not the sound of his return that awoke me but an eagerness for it. For whatever reason, I awoke often, knowing he was there, and, opening the door, would find him at his table, hard at work, still fully dressed.

" Come in. Don't talk for a bit."

I would climb into his bed and sit up, watching him; sometimes fall asleep. When he was done, he would begin to undress.

" Are you awake, David ? "

" Yes. Why don't you undress before you work? Why don't you work in a dressing-gown ? "

" I should feel tired if I did."

" Aren't you tired ? "

" Never."

" But why not ? I am."

" You wouldn't be if you didn't stop to think about it."

" But there's the night and there's the day."

" That's where you're wrong. There are twenty-four hours."

" But dancing—" I said. " What good does that do ? "

" Solicitors," he answered, " have daughters."

" Then you don't *like* it ? "

" I do, enormously. I should like it better if they could dance better."

35

When he was in his pyjama trousers, he did exercises.

" Now, off you go and sleep. And sleep *fast*. Most people sleep too slowly. They take eight hours about it. Four is enough."

Ann's birthday fell at that time. She and I had a custom of reading aloud, sometimes to help me with my English lessons, more often for pleasure. Her voice was true and steady, of lower pitch than most women's, and her reading had the sweet naturalness of her own character. Shelley was her particular god ; she had brought me to love even the *Skylark* by the simple process of leading me beyond the early lines which were my task at school. In a bookseller's catalogue, I saw advertised a " Large Paper Fine-Type Edition " of Shelley's poems at the price of at least three birthday presents. Because just then I was less near to Ann than I had been, her interest having unaccountably diverged from my life and works, I drew money from the Post Office Savings Bank and bought it for her.

I showed it to Howard.

" But I didn't know she had a birthday," he said. " What shall I get for her ? What would she like ? "

" Well, there are always silks," I answered. " She always wants more and more and more silks."

When her birthday came, the giving of presents, which had its customary place at breakfast, was deferred until the evening that Howard might be there, and there was claret (not for me) and Jubilee port (for me, half a glass) at dinner. In the drawing-room, presents, including packages that had come by post, were on a side-table. From my father, in an envelope, a five-pun note. Ann could not pretend to be surprised, but she put her arms round his neck and kissed him. She was in evening-dress for the occasion. I remember the ripple of her shoulders as she put up her arms, and Howard's smile.

My copy of Shelley was next unwrapped. She was rewardingly delighted. " Oh, David," she exclaimed, " but it is a special edition ! How wicked of you to be so extravagant ! " My father also spoke with approving irony. " Ah," he said, " you don't know David as well as I do. He is going to be the capitalist of the family." The book was examined, my loving inscription studied. Suddenly Ann raised her face. " Listen," she said.

The windows were partly open. It had been a warm, still day. Now the chestnuts were turning over their young leaves restlessly and there was a just audible whisper of rain.

I knew at once what was in her mind :

> *Sound of vernal showers*
> *On the twinkling grass,*
> *Rain-awaken'd flowers —*
> *All that ever was*
> *Joyous and clear and fresh — thy music doth surpass*

— but I would not for all the world have spoken, or have had her speak, the verses then. Our common recognition was enough. Uttering a little sound that was neither laugh nor sigh, she thanked me again for my gift, adding that I couldn't have given her a present to please her more ; she should always remember our reading Shelley together.

" I believe I really shall, even when I am quite old," she said, and I saw tears of happiness in her eyes.

37

They had come unbidden, taking her unawares, and to conceal them she said "thank you" again and embraced me. But it was not the kiss to be expected at present-givings. She was trembling, her cheek glowed against mine; for a moment her arms tightened. Suddenly she drew back, just as one does at a railway station when the train is about to start, and threw up her head and shook her dark hair. It had been a kiss of farewell.

"I have something for you too," Howard said.

At the sound of his voice she turned, I thought, abruptly, as though a hand had been laid on her arm, but her answer came with no more than a little roughening or deepening of her customary tone: "Oh, do let me see! What is it?"

It was a large, flat, oblong parcel, tied with lawyers' tape.

"Is this precious, or can I break it?"

"You won't be able to break it," and he opened his penknife for her.

The parcel contained a leather-bound book, much wider than it was tall, evidently a stamp-album. If Howard had asked me, I could have told him that Ann had given up stamp-collecting long ago. My cheeks burned, perhaps on account of his blunder. His present will be a failure, I said to myself, and Ann will have to pretend that it isn't.

Her silence, as she opened the book, confirmed my fears. I strode across the room and took post behind her, thinking that, when she did speak, I might make everything easier by helping her to pretend that she collected stamps after all. But the book open on her lap was musical script.

38

" Duets ! " she cried. " Howard, what made you think of that ? "

" I thought it might do me good if we learned to play them together," he answered in the half-serious tone which was cover to his seriousness.

" Bach—" she began and turned a page.

" It's not only Bach," he explained, dropping on one knee to her level, so eager to exhibit his gift that his hair came tumbling over his forehead. " It's a collection of duets, a kind of anthology. We shall probably find something——"

" If only I can play it," she put in. " You're much better than I am."

" I'm more fluent."

" You'll have to be patient and teach me."

" Oh," he answered, " I can teach you the fingering, I dare say, if you teach me what it's about."

She asked why he said that. At first he seemed not to know how to answer. Then he stood up, smoothed his hair back into its professional order, slipped his hands into his trouser pockets, and by the set of his mouth added ten years to his age. " Oh," he said, " because I'm not really capable of thinking in terms of music. From a musician's point of view I don't know what anything's about. Though I dare say, if I gave my mind to it, I could earn a fortune on the music-halls or on a concert-platform. That says nothing. I could be an enormously successful grocer — or a bishop, if it comes to that. But what I am is a lawyer and an advocate."

" A Judge, perhaps ? " my father said, intending a compliment.

" No," Howard said, " not if I can help it. It

39

isn't my job. My real job depends upon a power to exclude every interest except the one I'm going for, and upon feeling about it no more than one feels about a Queen in chess."

This kind of cool swagger made me stare admiringly because I so completely failed to guess at the weakness against which it was a buckling on of armour. Ann smiled at it.

" I don't think you would earn a fortune on the music-halls."

" Shouldn't I ? Why not ? It's a profession like another."

She gave no direct answer to this, but continued to turn the leaves of her album. " If you were as stony-hearted as you pretend——" she began.

" What ? "

" You wouldn't have——"

" What ? " he said. " Go on."

Ann who, in my experience, was infallible, seemed to have been taken off her guard.

" Don't cross-examine me," she said.

" No, no, of course not. But please say what you were going to say. If I were as——"

" I was going to say," she replied steadily, " that if you were really stony-hearted, you—" and her words came rushing out — " you would have given me some-thing else than this."

He took his hands out of his pockets and, coming to her side, began to turn the pages of her album, as anxious that she should praise his gift as I had been that she should admire my Shelley.

" You do like it ? I mean, it really was what you wanted ? "

" No," she said, and laid both her hands on the pages to prevent him from turning them restlessly to and fro. " Better than that. I didn't even know I wanted it."

My father, who had been at the window looking out into the darkness, now turned back into the room.

" You ought to give Howard a kiss for such a nice present."

He too had been infallible. Now, his saying that tightened the muscles of my shoulders and curled my toes inside my red slippers. But Ann did not hesitate. She lifted her face at once.

" Thank you, Howard," she said, and kissed him.

" Shall we try one of these — I mean — at the piano, now? . . . Or do you want me to show you that new step?"

" Show me the step first," she answered. " It will be easier to tackle a new piece when . . . by daylight, I mean, when we don't have to bother about the piano-candles."

They turned back the rugs and began to dance together, singing the tune, as there was no one to play it.

My father said : " I must go off and write some letters." I stood by the side-table and opened my Shelley, but I could not bring my mind to bear on it and laid it down.

" A *long* step," Howard was saying, " and a *dip* as you go forward, and then the other foot smoothly up behind. Heels almost brushing the floor. *Smoothly*, as if you had a tray on your head."

" I shall never do it ! " Ann exclaimed, breaking away and leaning forward, laughing, with her hands on her knees. " Yes, I shall. Come on. Try again."

She straightened herself and raised her arms for him to take her. The polished furniture and the floor threw up the blue of her dress, and behind her two sets of lustres vibrated on the mantelpiece.

I went up to my bedroom and settled down to work. After an hour or more my father put in his head.

"Hard at work. That's good. Don't keep it up too late. You'll be fresher in the morning."

I wanted him to stay. I wanted him to ask about the work I was doing and to show him exactly how much I had done. Work was our meeting-ground; I knew how deeply he cared that I should succeed; it frightened me to know how much he cared, and to-night I wanted to be frightened in that way.

"Father——" I began.

He had almost shut the door, but opened it again. "Yes, David?"

But there was nothing to say of all I wanted to say, so I asked instead: "What do you think Howard will end up as?"

"Ah, that's too long a guess."

"What is the top?"

"Of the legal profession? I suppose the Lord Chancellorship is."

"Then he'll get that."

"You never know. Anything may trip a man up. Marriage too early. Marriage to the wrong woman. An attack of illness just at the moment of his greatest opportunity. Competition is so fierce, not only at the top but all along the line, that he can't afford to miss a rung of the ladder."

"No," I said, "I suppose not," and pulled my table-lamp a little nearer to my book.

" Well, good-night, David, and God bless you."

" Good-night, Father."

" Sleep well," he said and added one of those little phrases of love that had been between us since my nursery days.

The door shut. I made up my mind to work on and on, although, if I also went to the Bar, the odds seemed to be against there being two Lord Chancellors in the family. In any case, to-night I would work on and on. I turned out the whining gas; the table-lamp alone would make concentration easier. I took off my dressing-gown and put on again my collar and my coat. Night and day did not exist; there were twenty-four hours.

Many of them seemed to have passed when I felt Howard's hand on my shoulder, but my watch said that it was twenty minutes to eleven.

" I wasn't really asleep."

" I know," he said. " I'll leave the door open. We can talk while we undress."

He would not let me go into his room that night but sat for a few minutes on the edge of my bed.

" You get in and curl up. I'll look out for your lamp."

" Are you going to work to-night? "

" To-night? Good heavens, no." He stretched and yawned.

" Then you are tired sometimes? "

" Of course I am. Dog tired. Why? "

" You said you never were."

" Did I? You see, if I find myself at a fancy-dress ball dressed as Oberon, I have to persuade myself I can work magic because———"

43

" Because what ? "

" Because then, perhaps, I can."

" Do you mean," I asked, pulling the bedclothes up over my left ear, " that everyone . . . more or less . . . goes about in a kind of . . . disguise, or that . . ."

I do not know whether Howard answered my question or even whether I completed it.

8

THE term ended for me in one of those drab periods of self-distrust which afflict the young who are older than their years and already carry within them a burden of responsibility for their own lives. I knew I had worked hard and believed I had worked well. When Mr. Libbett, by sarcastic asides rather than critical attack, implied that my work was in vain, I felt that my face had been slapped in the dark.

Whatever I say now of Mr. Libbett, or of myself in my relationship with him, is likely to be unjust. Within his mask of schoolmaster was a man I did not know; in my description of myself there must inevitably appear an analytical priggishness not present in the boy. Accept the mood as true; discount the analysis by which alone, after so many years, I can indicate it.

Mr. Libbett was a red-haired man, going bald. The hair remaining to him was short and bristly; pink flesh gleamed through it. He tweaked my hair, said it was too long and called me The Professor. This was my own fault. Once he had asked me what I wanted to become. Younger then and off my guard, I had foolishly replied: " A professor at Oxford." By this I had meant only what I was then incapable of saying — that to me classics and ancient history were an end in themselves. If I had said " a poet ", he might in time have forgiven me; if I had said "a clergyman", he would have hooted without ill-will. But a professorship was in his own territory. "Ah," he exclaimed, "he who would teach others must first teach himself." I had no wish to teach; I had said "professor" only because I could think of no other way of expressing my idea; but the harm was done. It was as if I had said to a disgruntled soldier that I proposed to win another Battle of Waterloo.

Nothing is more tiresome to a professional sceptic than a devotee, and I was an infuriating devotee of classical learning who had not the tact to conceal it. Mr. Libbett had decided forty years ago that the Romans used a code which, for the satisfaction of examiners, was to be ciphered or deciphered; my stubborn belief was that they used a language, and wrote poetry for pleasure and by ear. The contradiction was complete. Mr. Libbett had what he called "quirks" for dealing with his cipher. They were, for the most part, Ciceronian clichés ingeniously disguised. You learned them by heart and how to "adapt" them, substituting one verb for another, until each was a skeleton key to a dozen locks. You then fitted them in — as diners-out, carrying their stock of epigrams, fit each to its use. This was called "learning from the masters". Perhaps it was, and I a fool to hate it; but one does not carry gobbets of Addison in one's memory and "fit them in", or borrow a phrase from Gray and slip it, disguised, into an elegy; one listens and tries to write. I tried to write Latin, a dangerous habit. Mr. Libbett would tell me only that my attempt was inferior to Cicero's and that I might nevertheless have won good marks

if only I had not missed an obvious chance to fit in a
" quirk ".

" If you'd think a bit less about being a ' Professor
at Oxford '," he said, " and a bit more about keeping
on the rails. . . ."

The odd thing is that he was as wrong in thinking
me arrogant as I was in loathing his system. He was
trying to " get me through ", which was the matter
in hand, and I was trying to write Latin with an awful
reverence and an agonized penitence for my own
failures. Towards the end of the term, wishing to do
my duty, I produced a copy full of his " quirks ", too
full. The result was disastrous. " You ass," he exclaimed, " anyone can see through that ! You can't
lay 'em on with a trowel. You must use 'em delicately,
delicately, with a schoolboy clumsiness here and there
to cover the joins. This reads like a parody of Cicero."
Indeed it did, but if that wasn't what he wanted,
what did he want ? I saw no way out. I knew that
my own method was not good enough without the
help that he could not or would not give, and his
method I was evidently too incompetent to apply.

In this desperate mood, on the second day of the
holidays, I set out for the Manor. I say " in this
desperate mood ", for that was the reason I gave
myself. In truth, I had long known within me that I
should go, and went suddenly, jumping up from my
table, putting on my school-cap, throwing it off again
and going out bare-headed.

The Manor had always stood so much apart from
my day-to-day existence and had so legendary a place
in my imagination that my approach to it was not
easy. I might have gone by the Right of Way and

47

turned up through the park as I had in Mr. Letterby's company, or have taken a short-cut through the dingle which lay between the park and our own garden. Either way would have exposed me to the many windows' long regard, and I chose instead a circuitous route by our back gate and a small lane to the church. By going through the churchyard — a friendly place made friendlier by a parliament of rooks — I should reach a path at the back of the Manor by which Mr. Letterby came to Service when fine weather brought him on foot.

The door of the ancient church was open. Fearing that the Vicar might emerge and say : " Hullo, David, where are you off to ? " — and where else could I be going than to the Manor ? — I made haste to pass it. On my right, at a little distance from my path, was the grave in which Mrs. Letterby, brought home from the south of France, had recently been buried. A little dazzle of spring flowers, which I saw to have been carefully set out and tended, came up from her grave, and I began to compose a Latin epitaph for her, in which she should say : " That I was not worthless in all things, let the spring flowers and the love that planted them bear witness ", and would have gone over the grasses to read her name. But I dared not wait, and plunged forward out of the churchyard, seeing her in the picture-hat my father had spoken of and yet in her grave. How congruously, when imagination burns away their walls, do the rooms of thought run together in revelation, and yet in a way that cannot be told without an ironic smile !

There were certainly as many windows to stare at me from the back of the Manor as from the front, a fact I had forgotten, but they caused me no alarm. Since I left my house I had encountered no one, and I went up the Squire's churchgoing track with a buoyant confidence, as though I were invisible, with nothing in my mind but the sunshine and my epitaph. All was well suddenly. Every door would fly open at my touch.

So it must have been, though I remember none of the detail of my arrival until I was standing in Mr. Letterby's room and he, as though no time had elapsed since my earlier visit, was continuing our conversation where it had been broken off. The chess-problem was still set out on the table, the bronze lion still leaning against the tobacco-jar on the floor. I was given milk from a jug and biscuits from a tin.

"The point is this," said Mr. Letterby without prelude, "examinations are a waste of time except from two points of view: first, they can, if exacting enough and rewarded by enough privilege, prove to those who think otherwise that men are not equal; secondly, they are an incentive to learn. As intelligent men, we will proceed on that basis. What you already know, I will find out for myself. What precisely your Examiners require of you, you must tell me. Begin."

What was required of me I told him, but as soon as I began to say where I felt my weakness or strength, he checked me; that, he said, he would find out for himself. All that afternoon and the next and the next were spent in his finding me out, less by dubious inquiry than by the methods of a fencing-master who tries and tries his pupil, who yields, gives him opportunity, encourages his attack, and from time to time plucks his foil from his hands. Never had I been so taught; never so often defeated; never so little humiliated. In three days I had left my preparatory school and was at a university. I was stuttering in the streets of Rome.

My visiting the Manor could no longer be kept secret; I wanted, moreover, to share the excitement and importance of it. The news, when given, produced less effect than I had expected, and I grasped that for no one else, not even for Ann, was the Manor the legendary palace that it had become for me. Howard knew it by sight and name, no more. My father saw my penetration into it as a good joke. " Well, David, if you can get on the right side of the Squire, it's more than I have ever been able to do. You are becoming quite a courtier ! "

Hungry for my father's interest, I tried to explain how much help Mr. Letterby could give me in my work. This, to my astonishment, my father disbelieved. To him a schoolmaster was a schoolmaster and a professional; Mr. Libbett, he said, had a " real knack of getting boys up to concert-pitch ". Mr. Letterby he clearly regarded as an amateur who, to satisfy some aristocratic whim of his own, was probably wasting my time. " Still," he added on second thoughts, not wishing to discourage me, " you never know. It's kind of the old boy, after all. Let's hope good will come of it." The almost fatalistic tone in which he said this might have warned me that he, like Mr. Libbett, had decided that the scholarship was beyond my reach.

My opportunity to tell Ann came when I was alone with her. She caught the echo of my excitement and responded to it, but I knew that for an instant she had had to compel herself to respond. When her mind came back to me, she asked many of the questions I had hoped she would ask — about Mr. Letterby and the appearance of his room and how we worked together — but she was only half-listening to my answers. She was brimming in those days with a happiness of her own which I saw but did not yet interpret, although it had entered my mind some time earlier that perhaps one day she and Howard might marry. This had appeared to me as a conventional " family " prospect, not associated in my thought with any transformation of Ann or disturbance of that love between us which was the rock on which my life was built. She was flawless, changeless, invulnerable, the all-wise, the all-gentle, the near. Even now, after looking into my face, she asked the very question I most needed to be asked : " But tell me, David, why does going to Mr. Letterby mean so much to you? It helps with your work, I know. And it's always exciting to make — to make a new friend, if he's a really remarkable man. But you speak of it as if — oh, I don't know, as if you were Columbus and had discovered a new continent. Why is it all that ? "

I could not answer. Given words for the truth, I might have said that if you have the instinct of scholarship and are at a stage in life when you are burning to learn and feel the power to learn like a force of nature within you, and if you find a master who gives what you seek and takes what you give, who is seed and sun and rain to your earth, then your whole being breaks into flower. And she, if she had had words for her own truth, might have replied : as it does in the hope of requited love.

But I could say none of this.

I said lamely: " With him it's frightfully exciting. Somehow it works my deep magics."

" I know," she said, for ' deep magics ' was a phrase understood between us, " but how ? "

That day we could come no nearer to each other.

9

On the fourth day I stayed at the Manor until after
sunset. My father would be kept in London; our
evening meal at home delayed for him; and Mr.
Letterby dined so late — at nine o'clock, I believe —
that he was willing that I should stay as long as I would.

Once during the afternoon while the kettle was
boiling — for we brewed our own tea and fed from a
cupboard — we had gone out into the garden and
walked up and down under the windows, Mr. Letterby
with his chin pushed upward as though he were scenting
the air, his clipped grey hair whitened by the sun,
and his shoulders braced by arms tautened behind him
as though his wrists were bound. Rounding the corner
of the house and looking down its front, he saw at the
steps a motor-car, still at that time an object unfamiliar
enough to call attention to itself. It stood high, like
a waggonette without horses, its brass lamps, its railings
and its red enamel glittering in the sun.

" Now what is that do you suppose? " said Mr.
Letterby. " The Royal Mail or a fire-engine? Why,
if young Featherford wishes to sport one of those infernal
machines, he must paint it red, passes understanding."
A flood of Latin followed, so fierce that it sounded like
a curse, so fast that I missed it. " Well," said the Old
Roman, " translate ! "

" Would you mind, sir, saying it again ? "

" I will indeed ! " And he did, with even greater ferocity. " And I will translate : ' Who can take this filthy civilization of ours so . . . so damned calmly that he can hold himself in when the abominable Matho's brand-new litter comes . . . comes rolling up to the front-door . . . bulging with himself ! ' I'm sorry. We must treat Juvenal with respect. Still, allowing for my temper, it's the idea of the thing. Now come back into the room and treat it like a scholar." [1]

" What about *causidici* ? " I said.

He smiled his approval of my having missed it. " Matho," he answered, " was a pleader of causes, a lawyer. I said ' abominable '. Do you accept the synonym ? . . . No ? Well, so be it."

We sat down to translate. At the end I cautiously gave " full of himself " for *plena ipso*.

" Oh come," he exclaimed, " you must allow me ' bulging ' ! You won't better that. Even your examiners would allow you that ! And if they don't, may Juvenal haunt their dreams. . . . Not, I suppose," he added, " that they are likely to trouble you with Juvenal. Still, we aren't wasting our time. Look at *tam ferreus*. The conventional crib is ' iron-souled ' and it won't do ; but if ever you want to talk of a man who prides himself on his modernity and won't say boo to a goose because he has the craven fear of being thought illiberal, who holds himself in with steely moderation because he hasn't courage to speak out — well, remember *tam patiens . . . tam ferreus*. The

---

[1] *Nam quis iniquae*
tam patiens urbis, tam ferreus, ut teneat se,
causidici nova cum veniat lectica Mathonis,
plena ipso ?

Decline and Fall of the British Empire."

I was never to forget *ferreus* — or, indeed, Matho. The owner of the red motor-car was Matho for us from that day on, and drove me unknowingly down many a bypath of Juvenal. So in house or garden, with books or without them, I learned as I had never learned before.

After this interruption the afternoon had passed tranquilly. Sometimes I was set to write while my companion snoozed in his chair; sometimes we were hard at work together. Old Rapp, the dusty man-servant, had brought in two lamps to cast new shadows across the fading daylight, and the windows had begun to throw back our images, when we moved. Now and then there had been sounds from within the house: of bolts being shot in the passage which smelt of mackin-toshes; of music from a distance — a little jet of it, which ceased abruptly.

" For once," Mr. Letterby said, " she has graciously shut her door."

Later, there had been nearer sounds — a man's shouted laugh so explosively stifled that I could almost see a hand clapped over his mouth, a girl's voice, other voices confusedly, a scurry of footsteps and, I thought, the swish of a dress in the corridor outside the library in which we sat.

" Well," said the Squire at last, " if the twentieth century is going to squeak outside the door, we had better return from Rome. . . . Old Rapp has locked up the side-entrance. You go out by the front."

To him the elaborations of parting were unknown. Things that were past were done with him. He did not even watch you go, but became unconscious of your presence, supposing you to be already gone. I knew this too well to say that I did not know my way through the house. Gathering my books under my arm, I set out.

The corridor of the scurrying feet, in which I found myself, was itself dark but concluded in an arch of light, through which came a sound of movement and voices. There was no other way for me but to pass through them, and I went forward, my eyes bent on the illuminated arch, and yet aware, like a shying horse that evades his blinkers, of the black- and gilt-framed engravings which rose in glazed walls on either hand, the jockeys, the whiskered gentlemen in curly-brims, the hounds streaming in full cry, the bruisers, the bear-baiting, the cock-fights and the coronations. Voices ahead of me spoke together, were silent, broke again into little cries of encouragement or expectancy, were hushed again. I braced myself to pass through the lighted arch, knowing how the speakers would turn and stare at me.

The hall had a gallery running round it. A wide staircase on the right turned back towards me behind huge leather screens, gilded once, now cracked and blackened. In the middle of the hall, on an oval table, stood a cage, its gate open, its inhabitant flown. Nearer to me, close to the gallery jutting out over my head, was a suspended brass chandelier, partly visible, with three or four of its many candles burning. It was swinging. At the farther end of the room its companion hung, still and unillumined. The chief light in the hall came from two yellow-shaded oil lamps set on standards beside the empty hearth, a risen moon having no more effect than to throw into relief against its

56

pallor the frames of uncurtained windows in the gallery opposite.

The hall was uninhabited. I gazed about me for the vanished figures as one does among the ruins of a Roman villa or in the library at Malmaison; but everything was asleep; there was no movement but the dying swing of the chandelier, and no sound but the creak of its chain, high in the roof, like the wheeze of a bat. I listened to the astonished silence.

It can have lasted but a moment when I heard above me a little gasping, the palpitation of a voice rather than a voice itself, almost laughter, almost tears, and a man who said: " Now! . . . Now!"

" I can't," she answered. " I . . . just . . . can't! Oh! Oh! Do you think . . .?"

Launching out into mid-floor, I turned and gazed up. A girl on tiptoe was leaning out from the gallery, one hand holding fast to the rail, her body stretched forward, her other arm reaching for the chandelier. Her fingers closed on the air just short of its decreasing swing. At first I had no notion of what she was straining after. I saw only the perilous leaning, the brilliance of her candle-lit throat, her face eager and flushed, her parted lips, her wide eyes ablaze; and above her, like a huge quivering canopy, her shadow, stooping forward from wall to ceiling.

Drawing back a little, she said vehemently, looking to her right: " Don't stand there like a fool! Get the candles out! He'll catch fire and burn to death."

Following her eyes, I saw, above the leather screen, the long, narrow, horselike face of a young man blinking. Under her attack he threw his head forward, advanced two paces up the stairs as if to go to her

57

rescue, hesitated, repeated the gesture of indecisive bucking and came to a standstill. In that instant I saw on the central boss of the chandelier a squirrel, upright, clinging to the chain. Looking wildly round for some means of climbing to it, my eye fell upon a long pole lying across the floor under the chandelier. I threw down my books and ran for it, little knowing what it was or what use could be made of it — for the moment, it was no more than something to reach with — and found that it was miraculously a snuffer. Carrying it before me like a banner in a procession, I extinguished the four candles; then swung the chandelier towards her. The squirrel played his part, sprang on to her arm and from her arm to her shoulder, scolding her as she scolded him.

The young man, I became aware, had come down the stairs. Some other figure — that of another woman — was beside his, within a few yards of me, but they were outside the ring of my accepting mind.

I continued to look up at the gallery as, at sea, I have watched a new moon ride out from a cloud. She was standing at the rail; the squirrel was in her arms; I saw her only and the squirrel's tail curling up into her hair. The candles were gone, and the diamond-shine of my first seeing. Everything was quieter now, with, for me, an all-excluding quiet.

She looked back at me at first with a kind of wonder at finding herself so regarded; then, unaccustomed to the casting of spells so deep, she rescued herself with a smile of mischievous amusement — and indeed I must have been a comic figure, standing there with my snuffer like a halberdier, my eyes looking as if they had seen the Holy Grail.

" Who are you ? " she asked.

I must have told her, I suppose, and she have come down the stairs and introduced me to Dick Featherford and his sister, for soon the squirrel had been returned to his cage and we were all standing round it, she beside me, so that, as I moved, my hand touched her dress ; but so intense was my concentration upon her that I remember neither my answer, nor the introductions, nor even her coming down — the movement must have been concealed by the screen — but only her nearness to me beside the cage, which has cancelled in my recollection the lapses of time.

Not long afterwards we were on the steps outside the door. Daisy Featherford, with veils tied round a large brimmed cap, had climbed into the fire-engine. There was a clanking, a waving, a shouting, and a still night.

" I haven't really thanked you," she said. " I'm sure you saved Frisky's life."

" Is Frisky your squirrel ? "

" Yes, Frisky is the squirrel."

I wanted not to go. As I could think of nothing else, I said : " I don't understand. Why were those candles lighted ? "

" Just fun. They never are. We thought we'd have a grand illumination. You always have to give Dick something to do. He never has anything to say."

" But *how* did you light them ? "

" There's a little torch-thing on the end of the snuffer. We had just begun when I saw Frisky sitting in the middle of the chandelier. I dashed upstairs, and——"

" But what beats me is why he — Mr. Featherford, I mean — didn't put the candles out first and then . . ."

She laughed at that. "Well, he didn't. He dropped the snuffer and dashed upstairs too. Not very intelligent, I suppose . . . I can't have been very intelligent either. What do you think?"

This put me into a corner. I could not tell her that she was beyond the range of criticism. "Others abide our question. Thou art free . . ."

"That's different," I said.

"Is it?" There was a pause. Then she looked straight into my face in the light of the lamp above the front door. "Why," she began, "when you first——" But she left the question unfinished and asked whether I was the same David that she had heard spoken of as a friend of Tony Seaford. I said I was.

"Surely, he's much younger?"

"Only six weeks."

She reflected a moment. "He seemed to me . . . so much . . . all over the place," and she looked at me again.

I had a vision of Tony tumbling about after balls and swinging himself into trees.

"Then you are Howard Treladdin's cousin?"

"Why!" I exclaimed. "Do you know him?"

"At the Seafords'. He is — I mean, he's awfully intelligent, isn't he?"

I explained Howard's merits and how far he would go and how rich he would certainly be. I told her about there being neither night nor day, but twenty-four hours.

"Oh," she said, "even I can feel like that, but only when I'm dancing. Do you like dancing?"

"I don't dance well," I said. "Howard and Ann do."

" Who is Ann ? "

" My sister. . . . Please, do you mind telling me, do you play a mazurka of Chopin that goes like this . . ."

She listened. " Sometimes I try to."

" Then it was you."

" What was ? "

" You I heard, I mean, when I was working with your father."

" Oh Lord ! " she exclaimed, " I must have left my door open again."

Her never having finished the mazurka had endowed it, in my thought, with the evocative incompleteness of an unfinished picture. Like a fool, I questioned my magic. " You never finish it," I said.

" I know," she answered. " It's disgraceful, isn't it ? I always get stuck in the middle. And then if you know your aren't really any good, and never will be, it isn't worth— Why do you look at me like that ? "

I looked away. Clouds drifting across the moonlit sky were furry at their edges, and trees of the avenue leading down to the wrought-iron gate shivered and shook.

" Why, when I was in the gallery, and you first looked—" It was the question she had begun to ask before, and she broke it off now as she had then.

I was unable to speak.

" You don't know," she said, " what a frightfully ordinary person I am." And she added, as though she were speaking to herself. " I can't help looking like this."

I turned and looked at her through my absurd,

irrepressible tears. She was blurred and blazing. My boots clattered on the steps. I ran and ran; then stopped in the avenue and began to drag my feet. All my books were left behind. Why had I come by the avenue? Even though I turned out of it into the Right of Way, it meant a long trudge home.

10

Soon after this, I spent an afternoon at Tony Seaford's house, going there on my bicycle immediately after luncheon. Howard and Ann, it was understood, might come later.

The Seafords' way of living was more lavish and more modern than ours. Not that they were " smart " ; on the contrary, they were casually sporting and hospitable; but they had not, as a family, our small compactness. A host of cousins and friends drifted in and drifted out ; they so often overflowed their pew at church that it was a standing joke of my father's that the Seafords ought to pay a double rent, and every summer they had a private cricket week of their own. Mr. Seaford, moreover, enjoyed experimenting with new things. He had owned one of the earliest phonographs with cylindrical records, and very soon had had to buy another machine with disks. If only he had waited, my father pointed out, he wouldn't have burnt his fingers. Now he had a motor-car, a " hooting, banging thing . . . and mark my words," my father said, " as soon as a better one comes on the market he'll be wanting that. He just can't keep his fingers off a novelty. He's like a boy. A jolly fellow, I grant you, but no Seaford ever grows up."

The Seafords had not only a motor-car but a private installation of electricity from which Tony, his elder brother and sister and Mr. Seaford himself had profited to build up, on a table in the bay window of their billiard-room, an elaborate organization of bells, signals and illuminated railway stations for their system of steam and clockwork trains. Outside the house was a squash court and a hard pitch, covered with coconut matting, which enabled them to practise cricket in most weathers short of a blizzard. To all this there had been added during the preceding winter a hard tennis-court, of concrete painted green, which the whole family, except Mrs. Seaford, were contemplating as I rode up on my bicycle. They regarded tennis as a slightly effeminate game not to be taken seriously, but it was at least a means of exercising the body.

The court was as yet unused; the surrounding nets were not up. Parts of the concrete had sunk enough to hold lakes of rain-water; but as these lakes were wide and shallow, being nowhere more than half an inch deep, it was thought that they would not turn the ball. This was the problem being discussed by Tony and Hugh with their father while Marjorie swept out the water with a squeegee.

It was Saturday. For this reason Hugh had not gone to the City, where, since he came down from Cambridge, a comfortable employment had been found for him on the understanding that he should be free to play for Surrey during the cricket season. He, Tony and their father were in white flannels and sweaters; Hugh wore a Free Forester scarf; and Marjorie, a plain girl but as fresh-complexioned and as lithe as the rest of them, had made herself resemble an athletic young man as nearly as she might. I enjoyed their company always, because they gave me entry into a carefree world and because their cheerful method of laughing at me was to nickname me Julius Caesar and pretend that my profound scholarship, mysterious to them, was a reason for my laborious incompetence at games. I played up to this scholarly reputation when I wanted to make them laugh.

" Hail, Caesar ! " said Mr. Seaford, grinning at me under his puffy white moustache. " Now you shall tell us. D'you see those lakes Marjorie is sweeping out ? Are they going to spoil the court ? "

" I don't see why they should. They're so broad and shallow, the angle of deflection ought to be very small."

" The *what* ? " Hugh shouted, and they all roared at my pedantry as I had intended that they should.

" Come on then," Mr. Seaford said, " first we'll get up the nets. By that time the surface will have dried. Then we can test the ' angle of deflection '. Is that girl coming ? "

" What girl ? "

" Rose Letterby."

" She said she probably *might*," Marjorie put in. " You never can tell with her. And if she does, she'll really only have come to chatter and eat chocolate biscuits."

Her father pretended to slap her. " That doesn't sound too hospitable. I thought you liked her."

" I do ! I do ! " Marjorie protested, linking her arm in his as we all trooped off to the shed where the nets were lying. " I think she's rather fun in her own way. But if you expect her to be in time for anything or play any game seriously for more than ten secs. at a time, you're jolly well mistaken."

While we were putting up the nets round the court — a long, tiresome process with much pegging and hitching which could have been done in half the time if the Seafords had not all shouted contrary orders and periodically attacked one another in mock-desperation — I said to Tony: " Does she often come ? "

" Does who often come ? "

" Miss Letterby."

" Rose ? " He knocked in a peg with a mallet. " Now and then. Father and Hugh don't know what to make of her. Hugh goes pink and stares as if he thought she'd melt."

" Do you mean that Hugh——"

" O Lord, no. He's not such an ass. He laughs like anything when she isn't there. But when she is, he's speechless."

" And you," I said, " what do you think ? "

" Oh, I don't know," Tony replied indifferently. " Last time she was here, she actually wanted to turn on the gramophone and dance. In the afternoon. It was perfectly fine out of doors."

" Who are you talking about ? " said Marjorie, coming up to us at that moment.

She might well ask, for the conversation seemed to me to have taken a turn of indescribable queerness, to have drifted out of my reach and to be concerned with a subject altogether alien to me. This girl now spoken of was not she whose mazurka had come down to me from—

" Rose," Tony said.

Marjorie laughed good-humouredly. " Oh, she's rather fun in a way. She will try to talk to me about dress — to *me* of all people ! And do you know she saw some squash-balls on the hall-table and said they smelt nice and she wanted to learn. So I put her in old sand-shoes and took her on to the court and tried to teach her. But she didn't even try. You might as well teach an angel on a Christmas tree. She just floated about and laughed and waved her racquet ages after the ball had passed. She says she plays tennis."

" I bet she doesn't," Tony exclaimed.

" Oh, she may. Tennis is a Riviera game."

The nets were up at last and the Seafords stood back to admire their possession.

" I thought your cousin Howard was coming up to christen the new court," Mr. Seaford said. " He's a dab at this game, if I remember him at your place last year."

" He got a Blue for it," I answered proudly.

" Half-Blue," Hugh said. " There isn't a Whole-Blue for tennis."

I explained that Howard was coming if he returned from London in time. He had gone up that morning although it was Saturday.

" Chambers on Saturday morning ! " Mr. Seaford exclaimed. " The man must be out of his senses. Well, if he doesn't come, and Miss Rose neither, we'll make up a set ourselves. The light will be going if we wait until after tea."

As we moved in to collect racquets and balls, they all began to talk of Miss Letterby again in a friendly, critical, casual way which called up an image so different from my own that I felt shut out from their conversation and walked among them in silence. There seemed to be two distinct people : the inhabitant of the Manor, and the Seafords' occasional visitor who picked up a squash-ball and said that it smelt nice; to identify them was impossible. Even Mr. Seaford's praises were out of key.

" Well," he said in reply to some comment that had passed me by, " she may be rather a lightweight, but we can't all be Florence Nightingales, praise heaven, and I will say that a prettier piece of milk and roses I wait to see."

Never was a tragic princess more cruelly miscast! I burned as I might have done at an insult and a lie.

Dogs began to bark in the distance. In the intervals of their barking there was a sound of wheels.

" Hark ! " Mr. Seaford exlaimed. " There she is, after all." He smiled and rubbed his cheek. " It's like her to turn out old Letterby's carriage instead of hopping on to her bike."

As we stood to listen, I drove my clenched fists deep into the side-pockets of my jacket, pressing and pressing them downwards, willing her not to appear then. Although I could hear her wheels crunching nearer and nearer on the gravel, I had no doubt that my magic would succeed. If the Letterby carriage had risen in the air and vanished like Elijah's in a cloud, I should scarcely have considered the phenomenon excessive.

" It isn't," said Marjorie. " It's the grocer's afternoon delivery," and the sound of chariot wheels died away behind the house.

11

NEITHER Ann nor Howard had come when it was time for me to go home. In the past I should have been eager for their company; now I was glad not to have to talk, for too much had been happening on too many different planes of experience, and to steady myself I bicycled at a schoolboy's furious pace down the Seafords' drive. As soon as I was clear of it, I got off and began to walk, listening to the slow whirring of my bicycle wheels and the suck of my tires. " I must work. I must work. I must work," I said to myself, at first silently, then aloud.

Soon I came to the smithy and paused to look in over its gate, as I had so often done when I was a child, and hear the furnace roar under the bellows and the anvil clink. The smith was an old friend. " Days drawin' out," he said, and I thought how peaceful his life was and how secure; but, as we talked, he spoke of motor-cars, and, though he said jokingly that they'd always want horses to drag 'em home, I saw that he was afraid for his livelihood. " But maybe, as I'm old," he said, " horses'll last my time."

The responsibility of being young in an incalculably changing world came home to me as I walked on, and shook me; but I wasn't a classicist for nothing, and summoned to my aid, with young and faithful arrogance, the consolations of scholarship. That evening, for I had grown a little older, they worked less well than usual. Dick Featherford, I told myself, might be a threat in his flashy motor-car, but the threat became laughable as soon as you remembered Matho in his flashy litter two thousand years ago . . . unless, of course, you remembered also that the language in which Juvenal had written of Matho was called a " dead " language, and that all the poetry of Greece and Rome was lost, except to a few scholars. . . . So people said. But it wasn't true. . . . It isn't true, it isn't true, it isn't true, I repeated. Nothing is ultimately lost. If there had been no Greece there would have been no Renaissance. If there had been no — but I had begun to argue with myself. Always before, the value of scholarship had been for me an absolute and unassailable value;. I didn't have to prove its value in terms other than its own. But there are moments, above all on spring evenings, when the lakes that hold our moons are sucked into the earth and nothing is left but wine and the touch of a hand.

And if there is neither wine nor the touch of a hand, but only the whirr of bicycle wheels like a clock, one reverts to the ritual of faith — " I must work, I must work, I must work " — and, that failing, leaps on the bicycle and rides sedately (for it is necessary to keep one's head) out of the shadow of the trees.

At the head of Farthing Hill, I saw my sister walking towards me. For a moment I did not want even her company ; in the next, the simplicities and reassurances of my life returned to me because she was there. I dismounted and asked why she had not come to the Seafords'.

" Were they expecting me ? "

" You know they were ! "

She was not listening, made no reply, looked at me in an abstracted way as though I had no place in her mind. And yet she was brilliant, with her dark eyes widely attentive to something, her lips almost moving, her cheeks paler than usual and yet aglow.

" Howard didn't come back," she said at last.

" Where are you going now ? "

" To meet him. He's bound to come by this train."

I turned the wheel of my bicycle, intending to say that I would walk down Farthing Hill with her. From deep in the valley came the short, stolid puffs of a train restarting on its way down the branch-line. Its passengers would by now be outside the railway station. In a minute or two, if we walked a little way, we should see Howard turn the corner at the bottom of Farthing Hill.

" Come on," she said. " You come too."

The words were her natural words but the voice was not her natural voice.

" I don't think I will," I said. " I'll go straight on home . . . it's a fag to push this bike up the hill again."

It was the first time that there had been a polite falseness between Ann and me. She had not wanted me to go down the hill with her to meet Howard. For hours she had waited ; she wished to be near him and alone with him ; the colour had flowed into her face and she had looked at me with a kind of hot defiance that was at the same time an entreaty, wondering how much I had understood. Her kiss of farewell when I had given her my Shelley explained itself now.

When I reached home and had put my bicycle in its shed, I went into the drawing-room, which we used seldom. My Shelley was still on the side-table. I began to wander about the house and met my father.

"Well," he said, "how is work going?" And before I had time to answer: "Where is everyone? Howard not back yet?"

12

THE effect of my discovery that Ann was vulnerable was to make me love her for new reasons, and to fear for her, and therefore for myself, as I had not before. She became younger; I older, less dependent, less sure.

Until now, as we went to church on Sunday mornings, she had always been a part of the family procession, an institutional part, as my mother might have been if she had been alive; now I saw her with new eyes.

"Ann is wearing a new dress," I said to Howard, and he called out to her, who was walking ahead with my father: "David says you have a new dress, Ann."

"Well," she said, "so I have," and looked back over her shoulder with a glance that brought her eyelashes down on her cheek. "Do you like it?" Then she exclaimed laughingly to me: "What has happened to you, David? You have never noticed such a thing before!"

My father being churchwarden, it was our rule to be early. After we were settled in our pew, he withdrew from it and joined his fellow-warden to receive all comers. My place was next to his; Ann was on my right and Howard beyond her. It was my habit on these occasions, while the quarter-of-an-hour bell was ringing, to tell myself Greek stories (they had been fairy stories when I was younger) and to make great jumps forward in my own life, imagining myself at Oxford or making a Mediterranean voyage which always became pleasantly confused with the Odyssey. While I was occupied in this way the rhythm of the church-bell changed; a series of rapid single strokes said that the time of Service was near; and, as the choir-boys began to shuffle in, Mr. Letterby passed up the aisle, his daughter with him. We had all risen as the Vicar appeared. Mrs. Seaford, a tall woman with a taller hat, was in front of me. Though I mounted my hassock I could see nothing then of Miss Letterby; but later, when we were sitting or kneeling, a thin panel of vision, like an arrow-slit, opened up for me on to the Manor-pew, and through it I watched her ear, a lock of hair above it, a fleck of light that moved and danced but settled now and then, when her head was still, in a crescent on her averted cheek; and these things being enclosed, as it were, in a frame, which opened or shut with the movement of intervening shoulders, assumed the particularity and the detachment of a fragment of sea-shell looked at through a microscope.

When the Service was over, the Squire and Miss Letterby went out at once. The time was long past — and I personally remember no such time — in which it was a custom for the congregation to stay in their places until the Manor-pew had emptied itself. Now the village boys and many others " from over the railway " clattered out while the Vicar was still on his way to the vestry, but a certain giving of precedence survived among many of us. It appeared to be un-deliberate, but in fact we made no haste to move; Mr. Letterby always found his way pretty clear as he stalked down the aisle, and was generally gone up the church-yard before we were outside the porch.

This morning, as I came out with my father, I saw him standing on the turf a dozen yards away, a little aside from the gossiping knots of churchgoers. His hat was still in his hand, perhaps because the sun was bright, perhaps because he had forgotten to put it on, and, though he nodded here and there in an un-recognizing way, he spoke to no one. His daughter was at his side, the shadow of her hat — which must have been of a straw that the sun pierced with fine needles — giving to her face the effect of a lace mask. Her eyes, falling as I supposed upon me, gazed long and curiously; then, without moving them, she laid a gloved hand on Mr. Letterby's arm and spoke to him. He turned at once and came firmly towards us, and, taking my father's hand, to my father's too evident surprise, said with a glance at me: "Your boy has been helping me pass my time. Very pleasant I have found it"; and, when my father had made some grateful reply, he continued with a stare at Howard: "And our young people, I believe, have been amusin' each other."

There were handshakings and politeness. Howard and Rose began to chatter at once with, on his part at any rate, an ease that surprised me.

"You know my cousin?" he said. "Ann, you're an older inhabitant than I am. Perhaps you and Miss Letterby have met already."

"I believe we did," Ann answered, "as little girls at a party ages ago," at which Rose smiled and answered in a way that made me feel that she had not been listening to what Ann said.

Everyone except Ann was talking, no one but she was listening. A disquiet, almost alarm, arose in my mind: the same disquiet, though I had not then experience enough to detect its cause, which has always made me over-sensitive to that undertone of fear which a babble of small-talk may conceal. The babble has a cheerful sound, it seems light-hearted; everyone has a smile on their lips — how few in their eyes! Perhaps what I felt then was no more than an exaggeration of shyness, because others were chattering while I had nothing to say; perhaps my foolish vanity was touched because Rose Letterby's attention was not on me. In looking at Ann, my impulse may have been no better than a selfish longing for our old companionship — the same which, if I had still been a child, would have made me reach for her hand. What I am sure of is that, when I did look at her, I saw only her lips smiling, not her eyes; and this disturbed me, for her natural grace was, and is, of that gentle and serene order which lights a face from within, as sunrise a quiet sky. A moment later, Howard turned to her so abruptly that the smile vanished even from her lips, her dark eyes widened; but he put his hand under her arm and drew her so affectionately and easily into some joke that he and Rose were laughing about that the trouble left her; she let it slide away as though it were some foolish garment she ought not to have put on. Soon she was laughing with them; then talking in her own quiet, animated way, so that babble was no longer babble, and Howard himself was talking to her, giving his mind to her, and yet not forgetting that Rose must not be left outside the ring of their conversation.

I was outside the ring, but now untroubled. The

Squire took a pace in my direction. " Your father,"
he said, " is coming up to take a glass of sherry, and
see the ogre's den. . . . I don't know why it is, church
and sherry seem to go together."

My dear father was as pleased as he was surprised
by this advance. We all set out together by the path
out of the churchyard by which, composing my
epitaph, I had made my first independent approach
to the Manor. The Old Roman and my father led
the way, and the rest of us followed, now four abreast,
now two and two. Once I found myself at Rose's side.

" Well," she said, " you're very silent."

I turned my head and looked, and then looked
away — driven away by that invading beauty as
though it were indeed Aphrodite into whose face I
looked. I was thinking of three things at once : of her
ear that I had seen in church ; of the clatter of her talk
with Howard ; of my wild certainty that this clatter
did not represent her and that I alone, in my supreme
wisdom, knew her as she was.

I looked at her again and, because I was obsessed
by my visual sense of that extreme beauty, could find
nothing else to say than : " Why do you wear black
and white ? "

" Mustn't I ? "

" Oh yes, but you weren't in the gallery."

" Outside I wear it because my mother died not
long ago."

The blood rushed to my cheeks because I had been
so stupid as to forget it. Even then, instead of
apologizing as I wished, I floundered into explanation.
I had seen the grave and the flowers on it. On the first
morning, as I came to the Manor, I had . . .

" What ? "

" Nothing."

" What was it ? "

" Nothing . . . really . . . nothing."

" What was it ? "   She was ruthless.

But when I told her that it had been a Latin epitaph she was silent.

A long time later, she asked : " Do you mean, *you* composed a Latin epitaph for *my* mother ? "

I nodded.

" What was it ? "   The voice was quiet with the quiet of astonishment, but the purpose was unrelenting.   I stammered that I had only begun, I hadn't got the Latin.

" Tell me the English."

" I can't.   Really, really, I can't."

" Please tell me."

I could have lied, I suppose. . . . No, as I then was, with her power upon me, I could not have lied. I said : " ' That I was not altogether worthless, may these flowers and the love that planted them bear witness.' "

" Oh my God," she said, " how did you know that ? "

She took my hand and let it go.   An instant later she was walking with the others and I was trailing behind them.   How cool her hand had been under the lace glove, and how the lace had bitten into me its scarcely perceptible edges, its engraved dryness.

I do not remember reaching the Manor or leaving it.   I remember nothing more of that day.

13

It may have been on that Sunday morning that the madness, which even at its height he never ceased to recognize as madness, began to run in Howard's blood. He had seen Rose Letterby two or three times — more often than her casual reference to their meeting at the Seafords' had given me to understand — and passion of the kind that was to strike him does not wait upon slow transitions. No doubt the earliest impact had been fierce enough. Nevertheless, there is an interval between the first shudder of a fever and submission to it, and I would wager from my after-knowledge of Howard that his love of my sister, his intuition (which I believe never deserted him) that she was complementary to his life, his horror of wounding her, and, if I may put it so without irony, the foreseeing and ambitious habit of his mind, prolonged the interval in his case. He was young and poor. He needed freedom, not marriage; time, not urgent commitments; and, in any woman, a sure fidelity. He was so well aware of it that he is unlikely to have gone down to the fever of Rose Letterby without a struggle.

But after that Sunday the atmosphere of my home was changed. Outwardly it was as peaceful and active as ever and as customarily good-humoured. It was not in our habit to make scenes. Just as I, when hating my school-cap, had not flung it on the ground and trampled on it but had hung it on the brass knob of my bedstead, so did we all keep control of ourselves. It may be easier in the long run to belong to one of the nations who tear their hair.

Ann's steadiness was so much more than self-control, and so different from it, that she was still visibly happy. She had disallowed her fears with the same confidence with which men of faith disallow their scepticism. As light and darkness cannot co-exist, so there is a faith which puts away doubt, and a love which puts away jealousy; those who are capable of these things do not live in our fear of shadows; and Ann, having put jealousy behind her, was tranquil. But she had fought a battle; there were others to fight; it was a mastered tranquillity; and sometimes, when she played duets with Howard or when he went off into the garden " to take a breath of fresh air before I turn in ", I knew — how shall I describe it now who had no words for it then ? — that she was looking back upon that instant in the long retrospect of her own old age.

Howard, blaming himself for the indiscipline, admitted that he was not sleeping well, and it was true; I would hear him, in the room next mine, after we had settled down for the night, get up again and relight his gas. For this reason he took to walking after nightfall, sometimes in the garden with Ann or with all of us, but sometimes alone " for a good tramp ".

My father said : " He oughtn't to make any bones about sleeping at his age."

" Perhaps," Ann replied, " he's working too hard."

" Work ? Work never hurt anyone yet."

To me the indefinable change in my unchanging home appeared in my discovery that it was less easy

80

for me to work in my room than it had been. In the evenings, Howard, without wishing to do so — indeed, in his absentions from doing so — would disturb me as he had never done before. He would look into my room and, finding me at my books, withdraw; but I knew that he wanted to talk, and, if at last I went into his room, would find him staring at the papers spread on his table or writing with a kind of slow absorption, not now with the sharp rustle and scratch of turning leaves and note-taking which had been the rhythm of his legal work hitherto.

" What on earth are you doing ? Writing a poem ? "

" I ? A poem ? " Then he would smile at the expense of his own boasting in the past. " Even I shouldn't make my fortune at that ! "

He swung round in his chair and asked me about my work with Mr. Letterby : this, on the face of it, was natural enough. Then he would ask about the Manor itself — did I know what the picture was that hung over the chimneypiece in the hall ? Had the Squire ever said anything to me of their intending to sell it ? . . . No, of course not, why should he ? . . . But they did seem — if you looked at their lawns or their carpets or their paint, at anything that meant upkeep — fantastically poor. . . . The squirrel was a fierce little beast — and Howard would run on and on, always about the Manor, but never, except in some half-joking reference, about Rose herself. I did not yet grasp upon what point his thought was converging, but his unease was contagious; an anxiety, not for my scholarship, took hold of me; when at last I went to bed it was no longer with Latin verses sounding into my dreams. And it is in last thoughts and waking thoughts that the mind receives and hands on its messages. Everything is made in sleep.

Even by day, when Howard was absent, my room was not the cloister it had been. I heard Ann moving about the house and wanted to follow her. At the sound of the gardener's wheelbarrow on the path, I would go to the window and remain there, scratching the lichen on the stone sill, long after he was past. My tendency to idle frightened me, particularly when I found that I was treating the classics as I was well content to treat mathematics and French — that is to say, as a task, to be done with, one hoped, a sufficient competence, but tiresomely.

I went to the Manor more and more, for there the all-excluding hypnosis of work never failed me. But there was much I had to read and prepare without Mr. Letterby's tutorship, and though he seemed not to care how long I spent in his room, I felt that I could not for ever be there. When I began to explain this difficulty, he cut me short : " Try the card-room, across the passage. But you'll find no ink there."

It was a small room under dust-sheets now sagging with accumulated dust. Opposite the window was an Adam fireplace ; round the wall were chairs, super-imposed in pairs so that a set of legs stood up like tent-poles under each sheet ; above was a chandelier in a bag, and in mid-floor were four small tables piled with bulging objects under sheets. One of these I uncovered, and found a globe, an inlaid box containing cards and dice, a miniature cabinet of coins wrapped in wool, an inkstand and much else. Removing all but the inkstand, which should be replenished when I had beguiled old Rapp or brought ink from home, and

bringing out a couple of chairs, I settled down to work;
and this room, with its shrouded forms to keep an eye
on me, became my habit whenever I was not with Mr.
Letterby. I liked it and was at peace in it because
it was as rich in shapes as Greenland's icy mountains
and, at the same time, emptier — emptier, I mean, of
presences and memories that were concern of mine —
than any room I had known. There were ladies and
gentlemen in powdered hair whose silence, when I
stopped working, set me to work again.

> *Days and moments, quickly flying,*
> *Blend the living with the dead.*
> *Soon shall you and I be lying*
> *Each within his narrow bed.*

So my pen went on scratching, as it scratches now, and
I found that to write in Greek characters gave me the
same delight as the April scents drifting in through the
opened window.

PART TWO

THE LIGHTED WINDOW

14

Rose Letterby often appeared in the window frame, passing and, after a little while, repassing; or I would encounter her as I went through the house. She seemed never to have any destination. If we met, she would turn and walk with me a little way, then vanish with some excuse that she must not waste my time. These abrupt disappearances I considered natural in a young goddess, who might be expected to find me dull; it did not occur to me to wonder why she turned and walked with me at all, or to suppose that she might be lonely among the bleak corridors and the unweeded paths.

When she had company, she so eagerly made the most of it, laughing, calling out, chattering, continually moving like some graceful young animal, that I did not always resist temptation, but would leave my table and run across the room to watch.

" Oh, look ! " she cried, " we have brought Julius Caesar to the window ! " for the Seafords came sometimes and had taught her their own nickname for me. When Tony was there, with his elder brother and sister, his inclination was to " rout me out ", but he did so only once, and I suspect that it was she who afterwards restrained him, for she had learned from her father to respect the privacy of men with their noses in books. Nevertheless there was an afternoon on which, as I came from a bout of work with Mr. Letterby, the sound of voices drew me into the open.

Rusty croquet hoops had been set up on a lawn beyond the main entrance, but Rose and her four companions had tired of croquet and were on or around a garden bench near by — Hugh, a little bored, leaning against the back of it; Marjorie, cheerfully observant, standing with her feet well-planted in a man's attitude; and Tony himself spreadeagled on the grass among the chipped mallets they had thrown down. I passed Dick Featherford's motor-car drawn up under the great oak-tree that stood in the centre of the carriage-sweep, and at Rose's side was Matho himself, its proud owner, now leaning forward on a mallet-handle and quietly sucking the end of it. Tony Seaford sprang up; he had in his hand an old tennis-ball which he threw at me; I caught and returned it; he lobbed it, softly and accurately into Rose's lap — an invitation to join in which she accepted with such a movement as only winged creatures make. She did not rise from her place but had risen; or throw the ball but had thrown it, her body a part of its flight; and when the others were in a circle with us and the Seafords were flicking the ball from one to the other in a momentary game of their own, I saw her poised, her eyes grave with intentness but sparkling with delight. When her chance came, she missed the catch, but how her head and side swung to follow the flying ball, how she leaned back while the lumbering Matho retrieved it! The chance coming then to me, I threw her what I hoped would be an easy lob; it went a little wide. As her throat went back, her hands up (that should have been down); as she sped to receive it with a wild protest that it was too high, I prayed all the gods of Olympus to guide the ball into her hands. And the gods knew their own. In triumph, she flung it back at me faster than I could have believed possible, and, the gods being still merciful, I drew it down left-handed out of the air. Backwards and forwards the enchanted ball flew, as it did one day long ago on the shore of the Phaeacians, until at last it went bounding away into the deep, and a thrush came to inquire of the ensuing silence.

Upon the silences that follow lively activity, there is an accent of sadness. One hopes that the angels who pass are good angels, but is there not irony in their glance? The instant pleasure of being alive — the warmth of the sun, the flush of her cheek, the little hopping shadow of a thrush — intertwines itself with the long verities. Lyric and elegy are one. The shadow of her head is lengthened upon the grass. The thrush is gone. Hail and farewell!

Who is she, after all? And who am I? Everyone is now lazily disputing who shall fetch the ball. Nothing but a desire not to be thought a polite and dutiful schoolboy prevents me from going. She points a mocking finger at Dick Featherford and says: " Of course, we all know who will fetch it in the end. . . . Matho will! " and, for a moment, she seems to be speaking out of my own brain. How does she know that he is called Matho?

" Why do you call me ' Matho ' ? " says he. " Why have you suddenly started calling me that? Who was Matho? What does it mean? "

" I don't know! I don't know myself! " — but suddenly her laughter stops. Up the sloping ground, from among the long grasses, as though he were climbing a beach, my cousin Howard appears. He must have come early from the Temple, for he has been home and changed. The white collar of a tennis shirt is turned up about his neck in wings.

" Do you see a ball there — a tennis-ball ? "

" Where ? "

" Almost at your feet."

Anyone else would have had to wander about looking for it, but the gods have put it in Howard's path. He stoops and holds it up. As she moves towards him, he tosses it far over her head, and she is left with her back to me, her body stretched upward, her arms spread out.

15

It ought not to be logically possible, but is true nevertheless, that I should have been surprised, and even shocked, by Howard's admiration for Rose. The girl he saw, the gay, the flippant, the provocative, the tyrannical, was so evidently — so evidently to me — not the transcendent being whom I worshipped. Her beauty he could see as well as I, but he could not perceive, none but I could perceive, the inward and unique endowment of it. It is hard to say: but I thought her, in her social aspect, unworthy of him. They seemed always to be fooling whenever I saw them together, and I began to understand that, though he came when he could, it was because he could not resist coming. His supreme qualities in my eyes had always been his mastery of himself, and, within the sometimes arrogant self-confidence which that mastery gave him, his gentleness, his kindness of heart. In her company, particularly if Dick Featherford were there, he was fiercely brilliant, he would humiliate Matho when he could, and yet he gave me an impression of helplessness, as though, while he laughed and played and chattered with her, he hated the spell that bound him. A sensual passion always provokes hostility in those who are external to it; always presents itself as humiliating blindness to those who have not its eyes.

Outside the window of my own card-room was

another greenish area that had once been a tennis-lawn, now sunken into pits, full of plantains and couch-grass. Rose set all her slaves to work on it. When she had a playable tennis-lawn, not this year perhaps, she would give tennis-parties. Meanwhile, the weeding, the rolling, the planting of seed and the spreading over the seed of little strings decorated with paper kites to keep the birds away, became in themselves a party. I have seen Howard and Matho both on their knees together. She made the paper kites and entertained the workers.

Howard seemed always to be engaged, with a lightness of manner that was not lightness of heart, in asserting an ascendancy over Rose to which, with a dying flash, she would submit. So I distinguish their relationship now; at the time I was aware only of an unfamiliar tension between them; it astonished me that, in company with the dogged Matho, he should, so to speak, blunt his energy upon the tasks she set, and, even more, to see the fire of angry pleasure in her eyes when he rebelled and gave her an abrupt order, and she obeyed it.

He came to the Manor less often than Dick Featherford, for except at week-ends and now and then on a late afternoon, he had scant leisure by day, but he came when he could; and in the mornings, on his way to the station, he went now by the Right of Way across the park. How often did she rise early and meet him there? How often, and in what mood of anger or disappointment, did he draw blank?

There is, when one is very young, a special agony of understanding and not understanding. At home, Howard would say now and then that he had been to the Manor, having been " roped in to re-make their infernal tennis-lawn ", or that he had been to the Seafords' and had met Rose Letterby there; but he was not telling all there was to tell, and I imitated his reticence. It would be simple to believe that my reason was a schoolboy's unwillingness to tell tales out of school, and it is true that I was loyal to him. But my love of my sister was far deeper than my affection for him; in a conflict, I should have been ranged on her side; and yet I was discreetly silent without, at that time, a sense of wrong-doing, because, though the evidence of Howard's behaviour at the Manor was before my eyes, I had not given expression to it in my mind. I had not said to myself: He is in love with Rose Letterby. Perhaps he had not said it to himself. Knowledge and self-knowledge pass through a kind of purgatorial stage : one knows and does not know : one reads the evidence but does not proceed to the conclusion, particularly if the conclusion be subversive. So, when a friend dies, he seems not to be dead until the moment comes in which one says : I shall never again hear his voice or see the light of his eyes. So, when one loves or hates, the relationship is still free, still in suspense, until the moment in which it is defined by the words : I love, I hate. Understanding may exist, like rain in a cloud, without being precipitated in recognition, and, when one is very young, the interval may be long.

Besides, I was so engrossed by my own interior life that I was inclined to drift through whatever was external to it. I was carrying within me an image of Rose Letterby altogether different from that which appeared even to me when others were present, for little by little, in our chance encounters in the gardens and the corridors, a secret relationship had, I believed, been established between us. At first, no doubt, it was ridiculously one-sided, springing in her from little else than amused curiosity; she was willing to waste time on me, for she had time to waste; but her curiosity deepened and, in some very odd way, turned inward upon herself, until the moment came at which she said to me:

" Do you remember that first evening, I told you I was a very ordinary person ? "

" On the steps," I answered.

" Well, I am, you know. I just play about. You must have seen. My life is utterly and completely useless. I can't even play the piano."

" You could if you really tried."

" No I couldn't, that's where you're wrong. Up to a point — yes. ' Oh, my dear, how prettily you play ! ' Beyond that — no."

" No," I said, " I expect you're right."

She pealed with laughter at the unexpectedness of that.

" But it doesn't matter," I added, and she stopped laughing.

We were in a path, with a bank and a hedge on one side of it, leading out of the dingle. I had encountered her there on my way to the Manor, and she, as her habit was whenever we met, had turned to walk with me.

" You always say things like that," she said. " Why do you ? "

" We all fail at things. I shall fail my scholarship."

" Why should you ? My father says——"

" That's classics," I answered, " and even classics —
I may do them the way *he* likes, but examiners aren't
the same. And there are other subjects — French,
Maths and things — and I haven't done a stroke these
holidays."

" Why not? "

" Because I'm doing Latin and Greek. I *can't* leave
them. I mean, when you're in the swing — you see,
working with your father is something which — oh,
don't you see, I can't *break off* when it goes on in my
head all day . . . and all night, really. Like the time
last summer when we were in rooms by the sea, and
I heard the waves going on and on." From this excitement I returned to earth and my anxieties. " So I
have let all the rest go. Mr. Libbett says I get everything out of proportion. I expect he's right."

" I suppose," she said, " that's why my father likes
you so much — your Greek and Latin. When I was
very small he began to teach me. Then my mother
took me abroad. It wasn't my fault, but he has never
forgiven me for it. The first time we came back, he
said : ' Well, now you've been in France, try the
Gallic War.' I tried. I had forgotten it all. I stuck
at the second line. He just took the book away. ' Oh
well . . .' he said. You know how he says ' Oh
well . . .' in utter despair? That was the end of me."

" But surely," I asked, " he doesn't mind about
that now? "

" No. I don't suppose he does. I wish he did.
He doesn't mind any more about anything as far as
I am concerned, as long as I keep out of his way. I
am just a frivolous barbarian like my mother. But she
got away."

" Can't you ? "

She looked at me and smiled. " Some day, I expect. . . . Poor Father, he'd pay me to go, if he could. But Mother spent all her own money and more — oh, so much more ! "

In the hedge was blackthorn : first a tree in which the leaf had come and the blossom begun to fade ; then, a few yards away, another, by chance retarded, with tight buds of reddened bronze ; and now, where she paused and stood across my path, a third, made white, but not with the whiteness of snow or cherry, by an engraver's intricate point, whose finest line ran back down ribs of thorn into a cavern of pool-like gleam.

Above this thorn, against the sky, rose her golden head, shining, like a head of gold upon a shield. I looked my fill, and the sculptured head looked back at me.

But only our masks speak to each other, and she said :

" What are you staring at ? "

" The blackthorn."

If she had believed that I was looking at the black-thorn, would she not have turned to see what was behind her ? Instead, as I pressed forward because my moment in that place had fallen away into the past, she gave way and walked beside me.

We came out into the open and began to cross the park.

" I wish you could be there sometimes," I said, " when your father and I are doing Greek. I wish——"

" What use should I be ? "

" No *use*. But still . . ."

She answered something to which I did not listen,

so rapt was I in my identification of her with the beings who appeared to mortal eyes in the sea-foam or the mountain brook or the blackthorn-tree, or who, in the disguise of mortals, came knocking at the door; but I heard her say:

"It's a pity I am of no use to anyone. What do you think?"

The ironic lightness of her tone drew me. "What do you think?" was a phrase of hers, spoken on an upward movement of her voice, with which it was her habit to mock at herself. She continued rapidly: "You seem not to think I'm useless. Which is odd. You're the only one that doesn't. . . . But you are seeing something — I keep on telling you — you are seeing something that isn't there."

"Oh yes, it is there." I could say that.

"What is?"

I couldn't say that.

But now she pressed me. "It isn't—" she began, "or is it? — I mean, it's not just that I look like . . . what all the others see?"

I shook my head. It *was* that: the head on the shield; but it was also the holder of the shield, of whose presence her visible beauty was mask and emblem. I could not say it. I shook my head like a wet dog, as though I might shake poetry out of my hair.

To give me, I suppose, a kind of respite, the goddess then showed mercy on the blinded traveller and turned her face away. She made an excuse of primroses to go down on her knees and to say over her shoulder without looking at me:

"You are burning incense, you know. I shouldn't, if I were you." *Dixit, et avertens rosea cervice refulsit.*

97

I watched her gather the primroses and lay them stalk to stalk and cup them in leaves and bind them with long strands of pliant grass. " You hold them. I'll pick some more as we go up."

We walked on up the sloping ground, she a little behind me, but the second of the two shadows running before us told me that she was still there.

" What are you going to do this morning? "

" Latin."

" Alone or with my father? "

" With him."

" What Latin? "

" Elegiacs. Ovid. The *Metamorphoses*."

She had been talking for the sake of talking. When she was silent, I, wishing to be a polite man of the world, said:

" What are you going to do? "

" I? " She made no further answer; perhaps there was none. But suddenly she said: " There's one way I could be useful. I could read French with you. I could, I really could."

I turned at that. " Do you mean——"

" Yes. Why not? " she broke in, as eager as I had ever been to show off my accomplishments. " My French really is the French of a Frenchwoman! "

She was, incredibly, pleading with me.

" But I don't have to talk it," I said.

" In heaven's name, what do you have to do with it? Your English schools are mad."

A hunger to talk French had never afflicted me; one might as well talk algebra; but with her general proposition I was in full agreement.

" Quite mad," I said.

" Well then ? "

" Could you," I began with a strict eye to what was required of me, " I mean, would you correct a Prose ? "

She was delightedly amused by that solemnity. " But I talk it ! "

" I meant : written."

" I know you did, but—" Not to wound me, she banished her smile. " But tell me," she said, " at school, what French have you been doing ? "

" What books ? *Lettres de mon moulin* and bits of *Le Bourgeois Gentilhomme*."

At the name of the last, her eyes flickered at me, her lips moved, her smile irresistibly returned, and she began to laugh. " Oh, that is too good ! " she exclaimed, and laughed with such uncontrollable pleasure that I began to join in for the very companionship of it, without a notion of what she was laughing at. Not until late that night, on the edge of sleep, puzzling and puzzling, did I remember what Monsieur Jourdain in *Le Bourgeois Gentilhomme* had said on the subject of prose.

But now it was morning, and I was laughing with a goddess in flawless innocence of what I was laughing about. There is no more intelligent occupation on an April day.

She checked her laughter by pegging her lip with her teeth, but her mouth trembled still and her eyes shone.

" You see," she said, " even *prose* needs words, doesn't it ? And I talk them. Or we could read them. And you learn them. Wouldn't that do ? "

My feeling, not unjustified, was that confusion might result. But still it was true that my vocabulary was my weak point, weaker than my syntax or my grammar, and if I read with her . . . How long it takes to rationalize a surrender!

" Please say yes ! "

I moved my feet and observed that I was holding a bunch of primroses in my hand. " I am most frightfully grateful—" I began.

" Then," she said, " at least I can try." She sat down on the grass with her hands clasped round her knees. " I won't come farther now. You had better go on alone. And I shouldn't say anything to Father about the French lessons. He thinks it an immoral language."

" No. All right." I walked backward three paces up the hill. " Well, good-bye."

" Listen," she said. " Promise me something. I know what you were thinking. You're quite right: I can't *teach*. . . . At least, I suppose I can't. No, be honest, of course I can't really *teach*. . . . Still, I might be of use. But promise me: if I'm not, if I am just wasting your time, tell me. Promise ! "

" Of course."

" No, not ' of course '. . . . No, quite seriously, if — well, give me your word of honour. I have wasted quite enough of other people's time without wasting yours."

" How on earth shall I say it ? "

" Say what ? "

" If — I mean, if I did . . . want to stop ? "

" Oh," she said, " bless you. You must be the only really intelligent man in the world. Choose a word."

" A word ? "

" A word that will mean : I have had enough."

I clutched the primroses. "'Mazurka,'" I said.

She leaned back, her arms stretched taut. "Now we have come down to earth, haven't we? *Et voilà! J'ai enfin découvert ma vocation: être institutrice!*" She repeated the last word chantingly, as though it were the refrain of a song.

I let myself in by the Squire's side-door, but had enough presence of mind to leave my primroses in the shelter of a mackintosh.

16

A CERTAIN familiarity grew between Dick Featherford and me. It began on an evening when he had
come to take Rose out to dinner at his family's home,
which, I had been told, was at Melsdon, a village
beyond my range. A French lesson had been completed in Rose's sitting-room, not without the interruption of her waving to Dick from the window and
telling him she would be ready in a moment, and I had
come downstairs knowing that she had still to dress.

" How far is she on ? " Dick asked.

" She said she'd be very quick."

" Oh, I know all about that."

He kicked the tires of his motor-car, blinked at it
and bucked his head. Though he would grumble at
the way Rose treated him, I bore him no ill-will for
that; for I was convinced of her essential kindness,
and her behaviour to him was not in the part for
which I had cast her. She plainly tormented his
slowness, not so much ridiculing him as leading him
on to be naturally ridiculous, and she made it worse,
so far as he was concerned, by applying her torment
with so much good humour and with so ready a
welcome of her victim, that he was disarmed and did
not know how to defend himself. She gave him no
time to retaliate or even to be angry. If he stamped
his feet, she would call him " My cart-horse " and pat

him; and indeed he was like a great cart-horse vainly flicking his tail at flies. The cause of his undoing was that he enjoyed being called " my cart-horse ", which he understood, just as he deeply resented being called " Matho ", which he did not.

This problem of Matho had swollen in his mind and he was now determined to solve it. Moreover, as Howard Treladdin's cousin, I was an object of curiosity and suspicion. Of all this I was unaware as I stood on the steps of the Manor, but I was soon to learn.

" Pretty, isn't she ? " he said.

As soon as I understood that he was speaking of his motor-car, I agreed.

He stroked the bonnet. " Panhard. French make. That ought to please Rose. Don't you think so ? "

" I should think so," I said.

" Never speaks about it, I suppose, does she ? "

" I don't honestly think she ever has."

" No. I suppose not."

His crestfallen face told how desperately he needed her praise of something that belonged to him. This motor-car was his, his achievement, as my Latin was mine. He wanted it to be admired.

" She enjoys riding in it anyhow," he said hopefully, and plunged into poetry after his kind. " On a fine evening like this, bowling along the roads, looking clear over the hedges — why, in a carriage-an'-pair, if you go eight miles an hour, you're gallopin'. Can't keep that up long ! " There was a silence, during which he stood irresolute. Then he threw up his head. " Wouldn't like a ride, by any chance ? "

" But Miss Letterby may be coming down."

" Do her good to wait a bit," he exclaimed, defiant

in her absence. " Besides . . . come down ? . . . now ?
. . . Not on your life. Not with all that hair to do.
Time for a spin to the North Pole and back. Jump
up. . . . Anyhow," he added in a different voice,
" suppose she did come down. She wouldn't really
mind waitin' a bit. All that palaver's mostly show.
She's a good girl, really."

The noise of our starting, which was that of a shock
of cavalry in breastplates supported by medium artillery,
brought Rose to the window. She could be seen
speaking, but Matho in his motor-car was a different
man from Matho out of it. At the wheel, he was
master of his own fate and waved a casual hand to
prove it.

I looked back. " She's laughing," I reported.

" 'Course she is. I told you. She's a good girl,
really."

" Her hair was down," I said.

" Well, there you are," he answered. " Time for
the South Pole too."

After this, we talked no more of women, but of
machines, and of them little. We drove with silent
frenzy, beyond the forge, beyond the Seafords', into
the open, back again, and, after a great changing of
gears, with almost meditative slowness through the
wrought-iron gates. Half-way up the avenue, before
we were within sight from the windows of the Manor,
he stopped. The engine continued to hammer.

" Well," he said, " what do you think of her ? "

As the journey seemed unexpectedly to have ended,
I started to thank him. As soon as I began to speak,
he cut me short : " I wish you'd tell me something,
will you ? "

" Of course, I——"

" Well, it's this. When I ask Rose, she just laughs and says I'm to ask her father or you. Well, I can't ask her father, can I ? So I ask you. Why does she call me ' Matho ' ? Who was this fellow Matho ? "

I opened my mouth to laugh ; then, at sight of his face, peering in so anxiously at the absurd mystery, checked myself, and told him Matho was a lawyer in Juvenal who had a brand-new litter like his brand-new motor-car.

" Is that all ? I don't see why it's funny. . . . But tell me, what *kind* of a man was this Matho ? "

" A lawyer."

" Well, I'm not that. It's your cousin Treladdin who's the lawyer. . . . What else ? Was he a scoundrel or a nice chap or what ? "

Plena ipso : bulging with himself !

" Juvenal says his litter was full of him," I answered as tactfully as I could, " so I suppose he must have been huge."

This was thoughtfully considered. " O-o-oh," he exclaimed with a grin of relief. " A *big* man ! A big clumsy chap like me ! Is that all ! Oh well, I say, that's all right. Much the same as being called a cart-horse, isn't it ? "

" I suppose it is."

His hand went out for the gear-lever. " Fool I was to be worried about it. . . . Never means any harm. Good girl, really."

We lurched forward to the house in the highest spirits, blowing the horn.

" Only trouble about bein' big," he shouted. " I should like to go in for flyin' machines."

17

Nοτ for the last time, I was led by the affable pathos of a stupid man into forgetting the obduracy and guile of which dullness is capable, and was sorry for Matho when I learned, from a swift conversation between Hugh Seaford and Rose, that by Rose's insistence Matho had not been invited to the Seafords' dance. Indeed, the fact that they were giving a dance was concealed from him.

On the afternoon before the dance, having worked all day in the card-room or with Mr. Letterby, I made my way about tea-time to Rose's sitting-room. I had by now my own place there, in the window-seat among a pile of albums and illustrated papers, and I went to it without speaking, for she was at her piano, her fingers on the keys, and I supposed that she was about to play.

" You nearly let it out," she said.

" What — out ? "

" The dance. I did warn you. However, never mind. He's gone off quite happily. Poor Matho ! "

Having in my hand a translation into French of the opening passages of *Treasure Island* done without a dictionary, I rustled it a little, but, as I did not wish to demand too urgently attention to my own affairs, I said that Matho was bound to find out.

" Oh no," she said, " and even if he does, he can't

complain. His people live miles away. They don't know the Seafords. Hugh was only going to have him asked because he has met him here and he thought that I . . ."

" I don't blame Hugh," I said boldly, still on Matho's side. " I should have thought so too."

Her head turned and her eyes fell on me with that half-mocking, half-reproving gaze which by the intimacy of its challenge promoted me ten years.

" Would you ? What would you have thought ? "

" That you would have wanted him asked." I stood up and pretended to be looking out of the window.

" That isn't what I meant. *I* meant, anyhow *Hugh* meant—" It was the extreme emphasis that she used when explaining something to Matho's denseness, and I knew that her eyes were wide open like a doll's. " Hugh thinks that I am going to marry him."

I was deliberately stupid. " Marry Hugh ? "

She struck so tremendous a discord on the piano that it brought me round. Laughing in my face, she exclaimed : " That is an idea ! But I should have to sit on a leather cushion all day and watch cricket. . . . It would be a way out, though, wouldn't it ? " Then, moving from seriousness to raillery between the beginning and the end of her sentence, " I believe I don't want to marry anyone," she said, " except you ! . . . Then I shouldn't be bored and I shouldn't be frightened."

She came up from the piano and across the space that divided us in a single movement, and kissed me, so lightly, so glancingly, that there was no more than a warmth of her cheek against mine and the touch of her hair on my forehead, but the sting of it flowed up from the ground to my hair-roots and finger-tips as though a rigid and icy feather had been drawn over my flesh. Beyond her head, I saw a pendulum, with the face of the sun upon it, swing under the glass window of her clock. I was hooded and held in by a sense of my own absurd passivity, of standing like a frozen stick and doing nothing; so I put my arms round her, and kissed her — since her lips were there — on the lips.

Inaccurately, alas. But she had shut her eyes, for I watched them opening.

"Well," she said, and no more then. But when she had gone to the table at which we always sat if there was work to be done that needed pen and ink, I heard her say: "*C'est vrai alors. Je suis institutrice.*" Then she asked me: "Have you done your bit of — of *Treasure Island*, wasn't it?"

At about the seventh line I had worked in, last night, a piece of French — an elaborate use of the imperfect subjunctive — of which, when I wrote it, I had been uncommonly proud, but last night was already long ago and as I watched her now, reading my careful manuscript, I regarded even my imperfect subjunctive with a certain lassitude.

But when she came to it, she said: "Oh, but you can't say that!"

"Why not? By the sequence of tenses the verb must be in the past, and it must be subjunctive after *quoique.*"

"I haven't an idea what you're talking about. I have had governesses who talked like that, but I didn't listen. All I know is: you can't say that."

"But why? It's correct, isn't it?"

" I dare say it is. But you just can't use that word there."

" But why not ? "

" Because no Frenchman would."

" But wouldn't he have — in the eighteenth century ? "

" Not in the Garden of Eden. Though it does sound like a cartload of snakes."

" Well," I said, " if it's correct and I can't use it, what do I do ? "

" Turn it."

She turned it, this way and that. I had to admit that it sounded well when turned.

" And correct ? "

" Of course."

" And eighteenth century ? "

" Well, I wouldn't know."

" You are funny," she said. " You think, don't you, that because I chatter I can't be classical enough ? I promise you : my mother, who did just babble herself and was quite happy babbling but could hear herself making howlers — she had *me* brought up on Madame de Sévigné."

This too was, I suppose, pride in her accomplishment and, as such, blameless. Nothing is less smart and few things are more civilized than to be brought up on Madame de Sévigné. I was no doubt an inexperienced young fool. I do not justify my ingenuousness, but record it. . . . There was in her way of saying this an echo of the smart, loud-voiced throng, as I imagined it in its picture-hats, which had upon me, who could be easily shocked, an irrational effect of worldliness. Perhaps it was only a climax, not a cause. Perhaps the happenings of the last half-hour, and the impulsive, haphazard disproportion in which they had presented themselves to me, as though I had been in a fever, had to be paid for. Close to her at the table, I saw Rose in her likeness to her mother, not in her difference from her. Instead of penetrating her fierce beauty and finding solace in my own image of it, I was overpowered by its nearness as by too powerful a scent borne in upon too wilful a breeze. I felt that I was sinking. I was tired. I wanted to go away.

But my upbringing was such as made, in action, no concessions to emotional wilfulness. Having made an engagement, you kept it; having accepted a kindness from Miss Letterby, you did not change your mind; having begun a French lesson, you went through with it to the end, for, if you did not, the passage you neglected might be the very passage set by the examiners, and you miss a rung in the ladder.

I completed the French lesson. If she knew with how much difficulty, she gave no evidence of it. Perhaps that was in itself her merciful sign. When I rose at last, she came down into the hall with me, talking of casual things, and stood on the steps to watch me set out across the park. In the obliterating courtesy of that, she was the Old Roman's daughter.

" Good-night, David."

" Good-night, Miss Letterby."

On my way home I passed the blackthorn, but was too tired to worry about it.

18

ONE of the cuffs of Howard's evening-shirt had frayed. He was in his underclothes on the edge of his bed with a pair of nail-scissors in his hand.

"David, look, I may be getting late. Would you snip this for me and put the links in while I do my hair?"

"You can't do your hair before you put on your shirt."

"Yes, I can. This is one of my Cambridge shirts. Made like a coat."

"All right, I'll try."

"But are your hands clean?"

"Not particularly. I'll go and wash."

But my father, who also was going to the dance because it was his duty to accompany his daughter, was humming "Rock of Ages" in the bathroom. Abandoning Howard's shirt, I knocked on Ann's door.

She had dressed too early and, not wishing to confess it, was seated on an upright white-painted chair with a book on her lap.

"Come in, David. You are almost a stranger."

"What's the book?"

She hesitated a moment, then told me: "Roman Law. It's one of Howard's. I thought I might as well try to find out about it."

"I have been having a French lesson," I said.

" From Rose Letterby ? Can she really teach ? "

" In a way. But she can never tell me *why*."

I should then have told a great deal — I am not sure how much — but a great deal about my French lesson, if she had asked questions, but it was not her habit to fish in other people's waters. It was one of the comforts of being with her that I never felt she was trying to find out anything indirectly. Incapable of mental spying, she would not draw out confidence to her own purpose; and on this occasion she let the subject of Rose Letterby drop. Instead she told me I was looking tired and, when I had made the usual denials, added, with a long look at me, that I was going to be very like Howard when I grew up.

" Not as good-looking," I said. " To start with, my eyes aren't as wide apart, and my nose——"

" I didn't mean features exactly. But you and he have the same look of not allowing yourselves to be afraid. Which means that you aren't sure."

" Of what ? "

" Life, I suppose."

" But, Ann, he isn't afraid of anything. It's different for him. He knows perfectly well that he will succeed. He always has ; he always will. I'm not a bit like that."

" Nor is he. No one can be who isn't utterly ruthless. . . . He was dead-beat when he came home this evening. Everything was dust and ashes — particularly this dance. I think what he really wanted was to go to bed and go to sleep, or——"

" Or what ? "

She smiled. " Go to the Solomon Islands."

" What on earth do you mean ? "

" Out of it all. Away from having to be a successful

man. Away from having to shine at parties. Away from— Was he all right when you saw him ? "

" Why, yes, of course he was. Anyhow, he's going to the dance. He was dressing like mad."

" Like mad ? "

" He thought he was going to be late. One of his cuffs was frayed. I was going to trim it for him but my hands were dirty. I came over to wash."

My sister was unnecessarily repolishing her nails.

" Go and help him, David."

" It will all be done by now; he's frightfully efficient."

" Still, he'd like to have you there."

I did not move. " I want to stay and talk to you."

" What about ? "

" Oh, nothing. Just peaceful things."

She looked at me as she had when saying I should be like Howard when I grew up. My love of her, of her purity of heart, came down upon me like a calm ; I had said my prayers to her when I was little ; not always ; there had been nurses ; but sometimes I had said them to her, at just this time of evening. There had been a prayer common to us, too grown-up for nurses : " Lighten our darkness, we beseech thee, O Lord ; and by thy great mercy defend us from all perils and dangers of this night."

To-night she herself was troubled, so I stood up. " All right. I'll go," I said. " I'll wash first," and made for the door.

" Give me a kiss before you go." Not to-night, I thought ; but she added : " You'll be in bed before I come back," and that made it easier ; that made it routine. I crossed the small room and put my face down.

" Perils and dangers," I whispered.

This had been a custom between us once when parting at night. She should have repeated the words; then it would have been a custom still. As she did not, and could not, I pretended to notice nothing except that one of her shoes had fallen off. For some reason I picked it up and put it on her dressing-table; then went out.

Having washed my hands, I plunged my head into water, and went to Howard's room. His tie was almost complete; the buttons of his white waistcoat needed putting in.

" You're lucky," he said.

" Why ? "

" A night in."

" Then why do you go ? "

" Because I must. Because I want to." The contradiction of this appearing to him, he added : " I shall enjoy it when I get there. One always does. Besides, it's a treat for Ann. But what I should really like is to stay at home and play duets — which I do damn badly. Besides, there's a mass of work I ought to get through."

Collectively this appeared to me not to make sense. I put in the buttons.

He had such a splendour in his tail-coat and Ann such a radiance of party-going that dinner became a banquet; even my father entered into the spirit of it. When the hired fly came with its lamps golden on the fir-trees, I went down the steps of the porch to watch them get in.

" Well, old man," my father said, " you are in charge of the house."

I returned to it, went up to my room, and began to recapitulate my day's work. In my pocket I found the sheets of my translation of *Treasure Island*, and studied with curiosity the pencilled handwriting in the margin. I put my hand on the paper in the attitude of writing and, with a pen not dipped in ink, traced the letters Rose had made. Although I was not sleepy, it was impossible to work, but to go to bed so early would be a surrender. I sat in a wicker armchair with a book on my knee, and a confusion swam into my mind between blackthorn and the Solomon Islands.

19

My dream took me into a ship on a quiet sea. I was hidden inside a rocking-horse and looked out over the fo'c'sle through its glass eyes. From a painted sky, hailstones, faceted like diamonds, fell, and bounced on the deck. They struck the flanks of my horse; his rider shouted defiance.

When I started from my chair, still half-asleep, the wicker of it creaked like a forest. The gas-light blinked on the polished furniture. Everything in the room seemed to have been caught asleep and to stir resentfully. Another shower of pebbles against the pane splintered the silence and reawoke me violently, as though a thin sheet of ice had been broken over my head and shoulders.

When I put my head out of the window, I saw nothing at first but a beam of light and a man's boots and legs rising out of the garden path; for the moon was over the roof, this side of the house was in shadow, and the man had propped his bicycle against a flower-tub in such a position that the beam of its lamp fell low.

Wide awake now, I asked who was there. He said he had a telegram for Mr. Harbrook. How could he have a telegram at this time of night? Post-offices were shut. It was a railway-telegram, he said. He was a porter from the main-line junction. Was Mr. Harbrook there? Was that his house?

It was his house. I was his son. I would come down and see about it.

There was a point of gas on the landing, and another in the hall which I turned up fully so that I might inspect my visitor with care and, if he appeared dangerous, slam the door in his face. Tramps, I knew from report, had a trick of " putting a foot in a door ". As a precaution, and with a sense of mingled responsibility and adventure, I took from the hat-stand a knobbed walking-stick.

But the man patiently waiting on the mat in the porch was in railway uniform and so reassuringly polite that I invited him in and allowed the knobbed walking-stick to slide on to the carpet as unobtrusively as I could. What was required of me was clearly not piratical adventure but, as representative of the absent Chief Engineer, decisive action. Unwilling to break an envelope addressed to my father, I asked the porter whether he knew what had happened ; had there been an accident ? Was something off the rails ?

" Not an accident, I don't think, sir — not to a train, that is. A sub-*si*-dence I 'eard 'em say."

" Do they want my father to go ? "

" Well, sir, that I couldn't say."

I opened the telegram. It reported the collapse of a section of embankment near the entrance of Calsmead tunnel. There had been damage to the tunnel itself. This was believed not to be serious. Meanwhile both up and down lines were blocked, the down line heavily. " Situation in hand," the telegram ended. " Your presence not requisite. Hope clear nine ten ex London or earlier. ISFIELD." Isfield was one of my father's district engineers who had once given me a paint-box and was interested in pictures. For this reason, and perhaps for others, my father, while admitting his ability, was a little distrustful of it. Isfield was " a bit head in air " and I had not the least doubt that my father, reading " Your presence not requisite ", would twinkle his eyes and go.

I handed the telegram to the porter and, when he had shaken his head without comment, told him where my father was and that I would take the telegram to him.

" Then I'll be goin' 'ome," he said.

My purpose was to prove to my father that, in a crisis, I was neither a " head in air " nor a schoolboy. His object would be to " get on the spot " without delay. There would be carriages at the Seafords'. One of them would take him to the junction. How would he get to Calsmead ?

" Of course," I said, thinking of Matho and his litter, " what we really want is a motor-car."

" Them things, they'll take the bread out of our mouths some day. You see if they don't. Ruin of railways."

" That's what my father says."

" Do 'e now ? O' course what I says is——"

" Anyhow," I interrupted, " we haven't got one."

" No, sir, that's very true."

" And somehow my father has to get to Calsmead."

The porter was silent, bankrupt of ideas.

" Now look," I said. " You bike to the junction and tell them the Chief Engineer wants a special."

Special trains, I knew — for had I not attended the funeral of Queen Victoria ? — occurred on royal occasions ; there were also " Directors' Specials " in the background of my mind. It was a gamble, but it seemed also common sense, that the Chief Engineer should have one in emergency.

" A special train," I repeated.

" But at this time o' night there aint no trains 'cept them as comes through, and them's all stopped consequent on this sub-*si*-dence."

This was baffling, but illumination came.

" An engine, then. There must be one in the shunting-yard with steam up."

" There is that."

" Tell them to get it — well, I mean, to have it ready. Tell the — tell the signal-box to clear the line down to Calsmead."

The porter stared at me.

" But who's orders shall I say ? "

" The Chief Engineer's. Say he's on his way and look sharp."

" But spose 'e don't turn up ? "

" He will," I said.

Never before had I pledged my father. To have done so gave me authority over the porter and over myself. He went off with a wobbling tail-light, while I, remembering that my father had been wearing pumps and would need something stronger on the railway, collected a substantial pair of his boots, tucked some woollen socks into them, tied the laces together, and, going to the bicycle shed, slung them over the handle-bars.

There was a powerful moon, though an uncertain one, and I did not pause to light my bicycle lamp. The resolve to do without it was, I am afraid, not altogether the outcome of a rational calculation of the moon's strength. In taking out my bicycle, I was taking out my horse. As I swept through the garden gate, my sabre did unquestionably clank.

Nothing is harder to describe truthfully, because nothing is harder to reconcile in memory, than the conflict of boy and man in me at that time. My scholarship and my upbringing had matured me beyond my years; and the creature on my bicycle that night was thinking, or consciously striving to think, in terms of manhood while there ran through him great streaks of the imagination of a child. I was dramatizing myself as a dashing hussar, spurring through the night on a charger with nostrils distended like those of a rocking-horse; the shut smithy, as I passed it, served well as a possible ambush among the trees; the dance music from the Seafords' house as I drew near became " a sound of revelry by night " and I the bearer of news to Wellington on the eve of Waterloo. And yet, I was soberly wondering whether I had done right in letting the porter go, and in the orders I had given him. I had thought to save time. But what if my father wished to send a different message by the man I had sent away?

Still, the sound of a waltz through open windows at night is as arresting as the talk of a stream in a forest. You pause to listen, then move towards it, like an animal to water. As the house came into open view I checked my speed. Time would be saved by my not following the drive to the front-door, and in any case I was held by sound and sight. The Seafords' L-shaped drawing-room turned a corner of their house, and in two directions the parallelograms of window-light lay out over the surrounding lawn, like rows of double-

blank dominoes face-upward and luminous. Next to
the corner, and running longitudinally towards me as
I dismounted and wheeled my bicycle in over the
grass, was a conservatory, the inner door of which
opened into the drawing-room itself. Deciding to
enter by this way if it was open, as it seemed likely to
be, for there were dim Chinese lanterns in the conservatory, I put up my bicycle against the wall.

Two windows were before me, occupying with the
conservatory the base of the L : the grouped window
of a bay in which Mrs. Seaford ordinarily set her
tea-table, and its smaller companion on the farther
side of a pear-tree then in blossom. The other windows
of the room, whose outward shining I had previously
seen, were now cut off from me, for I was standing
close, in the crook of the glass-house.

Across the bay the dancers were sweeping, some
smoothly as Howard would wish, some spinning in a
Viennese waltz conducted in older fashion. The throb
of music came strongly from beyond the pear-tree, but
not point-blank, for the windows of the bay were shut.
At first the light dazzled me; I was aware of faces,
shoulders, eyes, lips, of the throng, its movement, its
pulse, above all of its lightness and its passage through
light which jutted out at me in bright flashes as the
groups went by. Only the upper parts of them could
I see from my level, but I began at once to recognize
people and to be amused by their unusual expressions
— the intentness of one, the open-mouthed laughter of
another at some inaudible joke, the gaze of a third
looking out over her partner's shoulder as abstractedly
as a cow over a gate.

Then an experience fell upon me of such penetrating

impact that, though it must have been fragmented in time, it has in memory the effect of a single, instantaneous pang.

The head for which, without knowing it, I had been looking, shone out as light through light, a golden uplifting and curling over and expense of light itself; and above it was Howard's face, not memorably his features, but their sculptural hardness, their look of stress, of fixity, of unseeingness, of being, in some unspeakable way, glazed. As this face was lowered, Rose's came up to the encounter; her hand moved on his shoulder; her eyes drew him down and down into herself as though she had reached out from the sea, and, when it was certain that eyelids must close upon them, they themselves were carried down, still wide open, by an inward movement towards him of that radiant head. The glaze closed over them both. The music stopped. Suddenly they were in the bay, a window had been thrown open, they were leaning out, together, over me. Small words broke between them, rather breath than words. With movements of hand or wrist or cheek that none other could see, they rubbed together intertwiningly, like cats.

My distinct impression of the incident ceases with the grip of my fingers on the loose handle of the green-house door. Memory is submerged in the thick, heated scents within and the yellow-ringed Os of darkness thrown down by Chinese lanterns on to the gritty floor. The reason of my coming flowed into me like a salvation. I felt for the crumpled telegram, which had become a talisman. The animals, male and female, had come into the hot-house. I broke past them with my head down and into the drawing-room. The floor was empty. Old men were herded at the mantelpiece, patting out the dead music with their feet. Everyone stared at me. My sister was on a settee with Henry Seaford at her side.

" Where is Father? "

" In the billiard-room, I think."

She did not ask: why do you want him? why have you come? what do you want? Others were curious and would have detained me, but I made my way.

He was standing by the model railway.

" Father, this came."

Intelligent as Ann, he read the telegram first.

" Who brought it? "

" A porter."

" Where is he? "

" I sent him back to the junction. I said you would go. They are getting an engine out."

" An engine? "

" To take you to Calsmead."

" Good. . . . Who told them to? "

" I did."

" You? Good. First-rate. . . . Seaford, if you'll forgive me and make my excuses, I must go." He explained what had happened, arranged for a conveyance.

" Can I come? "

" You come home with Ann and Howard."

" I want to come with you. Can I? "

Whether he grasped that there was stress within me, I shall never know.

" I brought you some thick boots," I said.

" Boots? Where? "

" My bike."

" Good," he said. " Find them. . . . Come with
me ? Why, yes, if you like."

I would not pass through the drawing-room again
but made a long circuit of the house. In five minutes
I was driving away at my father's side.

" What have you done with your bike ? "

" Left it."

" Where ? "

" Outside the greenhouse."

" It will rust," he said. " There'll be a heavy
dew. . . . You should take care of your things, David.
They all cost money."

But he was pleased with me that night. I was
listening to the clop of the horse's hooves, glad that
our journey was to be long.

" That Letterby girl," my father said, " takes after
her mother."

" Was the Squire there ? " I asked.

" Too much sense. . . . Tired, David ? "

" No."

" Easily put you down. You could slip home."

" No. No. You said I could come with you."

I didn't want to be at home when Ann and Howard
came back together.

My father argued no more. He was leaning down
to the dark floor of the cab, feeling for the boots I had
brought him.

" Socks, too," he said.

" Yes."

" Good of you to remember them."

20

Dᴜʀɪɴɢ the two days that followed these adventures
I lay in bed with a harmless temperature caused, I
suppose, by excitement and want of sleep. They were
eventless days. My father and Howard looked in now
and then, Ann brought me a tray and sometimes
remained with her embroidery. No one spoke of the
Seafords' dance, but no one, except my father, thought
of much else. Howard treated Ann with an avoiding
gentleness, as though he had struck her, and even my
father, in whom personal comment was extremely rare,
said that she looked tired. " Oh no," she answered,
" I'm perfectly all right," but she drew her lip in
under her teeth and held it there, a thing she had
never done before.

In these circumstances to be inactive was unbearable. I felt that a cold, excluding mist had arisen
between me and life and that I must at all costs
penetrate it. On the third morning I got up, trying
to believe that everything would become normal again
if I behaved normally and did my work and went
about as usual, but it was not so. In Mr. Letterby's
room nothing was changed, but when, returning across
the park, I saw Rose at a little distance and my heart
leapt, I turned aside in the next instant to avoid her,
knowing that, if we met, she would speak to me, as
Howard and Ann did now, in an abstracted way, and

look through me out of a trouble, a fire, an obsession, in which I had no part. I began to feel that I had no place anywhere, that I had become invisible. Certainly, if I were so foolish as to go to her room for a French lesson, she would wonder why I had come.

The holidays ended and my daily routine of school-going began again. It was summer routine — that is to say, there were two periods of work after luncheon, then cricket. Before the Seafords' dance I had persuaded my father to intervene with Mr. Libbett so that I might be excused cricket and, except on the days of Mr. Libbett's own scholarship class, be able to return home at tea-time. After a formidable resistance, Mr. Libbett, from whom my purpose to work at the Manor was discreetly hidden, had yielded, and at the end of each afternoon-school I was free. Now I almost regretted it. My home had withdrawn from me. I did not know what was going on and could not ask. Howard was frozen and anxious; Ann suffering; but the nature of her suffering was mysterious to me, for jealousy as I understood it from Shakespeare was fierce and retaliatory, and she neither. The tension in Howard was that of repressed fever; in her, of an anguished faith that I could not then guess at. But the double stress bore me down. I envied the books on their shelves because they were unconscious and unchanged, and wondered as I hung out of the morning-room window, while Ann, in a chair behind me, stared at the book of which she so seldom turned a page, how it was that the blackbird sang so naturally.

The remedy was work, the impersonal passion, the everlasting solace. With Mr. Letterby I could apply it almost as I had done in the past, but not in solitude.

In the card-room at the Manor or in my own bedroom, work became a frenzy of concentration invaded by anxiety. If I looked up from my book, I would see myself in some vast examination hall with blank paper before me on which I had nothing to write. Or I would wonder whether, in my scorn of Mr. Libbett and his " quirks ", I was being an arrogant fool and throwing away my last chances. Perhaps my devotion to the Squire was mere vanity and crankiness, and, from the point of view of my scholarship, a waste of time? Perhaps what I needed was cramming, not leisurely, peaceful, selfless scholarship of the Squire's kind? I began to distrust myself and him. . . . And what of my French? Was I so sure of it? At school we laboured at grammar and syntax as if we were putting together the inanimate pieces of a machine, always within the saving insularity of our idea, to which our master subscribed, that French was in any case an effeminate and slightly ridiculous exercise, like hockey or dancing, which bore upon it the stigma of illegitimacy. I had always known that this was nonsense, but Rose had been the first to make me *feel* that it was so. Not that she was a scholar of French, but she took it for granted as a source of civilization and grace. To use it ill was not, for her, a reason for insular back-patting, but a barbarism to be laughed at. Besides, she gave me what I most needed : vocabulary and idiom.

One morning, as I sat in the card-room over my Greek, my not going to her any more appeared as an absurd schoolboyish shyness which I was allowing to destroy my gambler's chance of a scholarship. After all, she didn't know that I had watched her dancing with Howard. Why should her behaviour to me be changed? There were less than five weeks before I must sit for my exam. As I counted them, shyness, as shyness often does, converted itself into an urgent and extreme boldness. Greek was thrust away; with Napoleonic abruptness — ruthlessness was, perhaps, the romantic word — I rose from the table, opened the door, banged it, and strode along the passage — imperiously.

How is it that as one grows old one can, at the same time, dramatize oneself and laugh inwardly at the dramatization? Perhaps the great tycoons do not; perhaps that is why they are great tycoons. Certainly I was at the moment solemn enough, but my imperious mood did not last: I stopped striding; and as I crossed the hall and went up the stairs towards the gallery in which I had first seen her, my own nature returned and I said to myself, standing on one leg while the other hovered between one stair and the next: I shall knock on the door, her voice will answer, and I shall be in the same room with her again. I pulled my wrist across my eyes to wipe away that dazzling blindness.

"You!" she said when I stood in the open door, and she turned back to the squirrel in her hands.

"But perhaps you're busy," I began.

"Busy? I'm bored to death. Why?"

"I thought . . . perhaps . . . French?"

The idea came up to her like a bucket from a deep well. She put the squirrel back into its cage, which was on the floor beside her couch, with an indescribable air of having dropped the squirrel out of her mind, back into the well from which the idea of French had so unexpectedly emerged. In doing so she turned her head away and lowered it, revealing her neck's whiteness in the high secret place under her hair, and, as I waited for her eyes' return, already holding in my mind as a breathless memory the glowing cheek that I had been touching with sight a second ago, she began to speak French in a tone at once declamatory and mocking, and so fast that I understood not a word of it. Then her face came round ; she straightened her body on the couch, spoke on and on with arms outstretched and an ever more exaggerated stress, ten, twenty, thirty lines perhaps, a wild patter of alexandrines, then stopped as a bird does that flies into a pane of glass.

" What was that ? " I asked politely.

" I don't know," she answered, and I think that, by the time she gave it, the answer had become true.

" So Julius Caesar," she said, " has come for his French lesson. Then a French lesson there shall be."

" Not if I'm in the way. Am I ? "

" No, David, you are not. Thank heaven you came. What were we reading ? "

" There were two books," I replied, " the *Mémoires d'outre-tombe* and the *Princesse de Clèves*. We tried both. We hadn't finished either."

" Finished ? " She smiled at that and then added with a spontaneous tenderness that was like a summer's night when the eyes begin to see again after the glitter of fireworks : " We never shall finish them, I suppose. To read a book one will never finish — that's a dark thought, isn't it ? "

Her whole manner was changed. I could hear her thinking : I have been cruel and silly. She was determined to behave well, to be useful, to do her duty,

129

and took down the *Princesse de Clèves* with a determined upstretching of body and arm, and a flick of her finger to bring it from its shelf. It fell. We stooped together, touched, separated without laughing. As there was but one copy, we sat side by side in the window-seat, and I began to read, then to translate. She paid strict attention. Now and then she did what was of great value to me — covered the page, invented an English sentence related in form to one I had been reading in French, and demanded of me a translation in the manner of Madame de Lafayette. I responded eagerly at first, but it was a June morning and the window was open. The sweet air went to my head, the sun slanted down upon her hand pressed on the chintz between us, and the moment, suddenly, as one that would never come again, laid its silence upon me. But I struggled on. I abstained from looking at her face because the experience I was living through was of her total presence, of my being held in the same light with her; it did not require the particularity of her face; and I struggled on with the printed page, still careful of my accent. At the end of the paragraph I went back to translate. When, in difficulty, I paused for her help, none came. Then I looked, and, as my face came up, she jerked her attention back. " Oh, David, I'm sorry; say that bit again! " and she compelled her mind to me. So for a little while.

It was no good. Before long another silence fell and this time she said quietly, meeting my eyes:

" I'm sorry. I can't." And then, with a movement of her hand that did not touch me, the one word: " Mazurka ".

For an instant, I did not understand. I had forgotten the code-word arranged between us in another age — Mazurka : I have had enough. But I remembered in time. The rule was to ask no questions, not to argue, not to make a scene, to let go. I wanted her to understand that I knew this and was not hurt or indignant because she could not continue our French lessons, and yet I could find nothing to say. So I closed the *Princesse de Clèves* and gave it back into her hands, then knelt on the window-seat and leaned out. There was a blackbird singing near and a cuckoo far off across the park. After a few moments, I went from the room as ordinarily as I could. I thought she might cry or laugh, and I dreaded it ; but she played her part and had not moved when I shut the door.

21

SUNDAYS in my home were by no means the days of gloom and repression which are often depicted in modern accounts of the period, but they were made to differ from week-days in every way possible. We breakfasted at nine, not eight; there was brown bread, not white, and coffee instead of tea. We all wore different clothes; the maids had prettier caps and aprons and put them on earlier in the day, presumably because little housework was done after breakfast that morning. After midday dinner, at which there was glass and silver not ordinarily used and a table-cloth with such stiff, new creases in it as would tilt a wine-glass incautiously placed, we would spend the afternoon " basking ". No games were played, no gardening was permitted, no form of physical exercise except walking was undertaken, but if you had work to do — Howard's briefs or my scholarship or my father's own plans — why, then you must do it, for work, which made for advancement or in his own case for the better service of the railway, was in my father's view sacred; the most Sabbatarian of deities would not object to it; but Ann, though she might embroider, might not make clothes. The sewing-machine was put away.

" Bask " was my father's word, and indeed if I were to trust my recollection I should suppose that there must have been, in the early years of the century, an astonishing number of hot Sundays under a clear sky. Winter days I recall, but no winter Sundays : " eternal summer gilds them yet ". I remember them from May to September as periods of tranquillity in which nothing was louder than a pigeon or more startling than the thud of an apple. There was no sanctimonious hush, but I believe it to be true that we talked more quietly than at other times and always of peaceful subjects. Nothing happened that was not in the order of things. My father resisted the temptation of politics — except parish politics when the Vicar came to tea. There was no newspaper. Personal controversy was avoided. " Six days a week," my father would say, " are enough to quarrel in."

It was therefore a shock when one Sunday morning, which must have been early in June, controversy broke out stridently. The energy of my father's intervention made it clear to me that he was better aware of the stress between Ann and Howard and Rose Letterby than I had supposed.

On the preceding afternoon we had given our first tennis-party of that year. The side of the lawns had been crowded. Rose had come, the Seafords and many others. There had been tea and home-made ices of legendary creaminess, and lemonade, and claret-cup in red glasses, and Ann's cakes. My father, who was a good player and a genial host, had enjoyed himself. He had even chosen Rose as his partner in one set, and " just to prove ", as he said " that the young fellows don't have it all their own way ", he had determined to win and had won. His strategy was to keep her, as he kept all ladies, well outside the back-line in the hope of a return now and then, but to win by

133

his own service and on the net. That she had on occasions a severe forehand drive, which she would follow up in expectation of a volley, recommended her in practice but not in theory. When she scored a point off her own racquet by these unfeminine methods his applause was Tuscan.

Acting as ball-boy during this set, I found my father unusually conversational. He asked whether she found it dull in Letterby, " where I'm afraid there aren't many parties for young people "; he said how kind it was of her " to teach my youngster French "; and he hazarded, as though she were foreign, that perhaps she found it " a bit strange at first, living in England ". The questions led her to chatter volubly and nervously. When she chattered he said no more than was necessary to lead her on again after the interruption of a stroke. It dawned upon me that she was being adroitly cross-examined. Howard, on the side-line, was anxiously observing the process.

It was at tea-time that I received my first hint of a river picnic. I was loitering on the edge of a group of which Rose was one, with a tray of ices in my hands.

" But at Slipton," she said to Marjorie Seaford, " there used to be punts? My mother had one there ages ago. I remember huge red cushions with tassels."

" There *used* to be," Marjorie replied stolidly. " We sold ours."

" Why ? "

" Hardly ever used it."

" But why ? "

Marjorie grinned. " Well, we're not as a family given to lolling."

" You needn't loll," Rose said. " You can punt and I shall loll."

She had made up her mind. Punts would be hired. Henry Seaford should organize the expedition. They would all bring hampers.

" Carry them ? " Howard protested, and she decided that Matho and his sister must come because they had a car. Then she turned to Ann and presented her with a *fait accompli*.

" We are all going to Slipton for a river picnic."

" When ? "

Rose didn't know. " To-day week ? To-day fortnight ? Is it a good idea ? "

" I can't punt," said Ann.

" That doesn't matter. There are lots of men : Henry, Tony, Dick Featherford, Howard, David." Her face lighted up. " That makes six — with Marjorie ! "

Marjorie let out one of her cheerful guffaws. " Do we swim ? "

" Not," said Howard, " voluntarily."

Rose looked at him, bewildered. Matho, had he been there, might have said : " Not if we don't fall in from the end of a punt-pole," and would have announced his humour with a bellow, to which she would have gaily responded ; but Howard's single word was too swift for her. There are minds that cannot jump a step. While Ann smiled and began to move away, Rose, having missed the point, threw at Howard a glance of almost angry entreaty.

" I haven't a notion what you're talking about. . . . But, Ann," she exclaimed, " you will come ? It would be such fun. . . . Make her, Howard ! "

" Of course she will come," Howard said.

" Yes," Ann answered, " I should like to, if it really happens."

That trivial conversation remains in my mind as the recollection of a battle remains, perhaps, in the mind of a private soldier who, at the time, understood little of it and yet felt the great yawn of history at the passion of mortal fools. Why had Howard said : " Of course she will come " ? Why had Ann, who knew her own mind, agreed ? Why had Rose been frightened by what had seemed to me nothing but Howard's habitual quickness of retort ? Why did I myself tremble as I held out my silly tray of ices and no one took the least notice of them ?

On Sunday, as luncheon ended and the time for " basking " drew near, Howard asked my father why no one went punting at Slipton now.

" I believe the Slipton people do. Some went from here in times past. The Seafords did. I never cared for it. You get the water up your sleeves."

" Well," said Howard, " that isn't compulsory. . . . Henry's going to revive it."

" Henry ? Henry who ? Revive what ? "

" Punting. . . . Henry Seaford."

" Oh, is he ? "

At this point my father became aware that something was about to be said that he did not wish to hear. He made it difficult by twisting his port-glass to and fro and asking Ann what she proposed to do this afternoon. But she gave him no help.

" Read, I think," she said.

" We are all going to have a river picnic next Saturday," Howard continued.

" All ? "

" Three Seafords. We three — that's six. Two Featherfords. And Miss Letterby's coming."

" Tea, I suppose."

" No, supper."

" David here, out of doors all night ? Never heard of such a thing. Last time that happened you remember the consequence. Three days in bed."

" Two," I said.

" That's no matter. Here is David's exam coming on. He must be given every chance."

" If you feel like that," said Howard, " I suppose we could leave David out."

To this my father for some time made no answer except: " That's not the point and quite well you know it." Then he added : " This is a quiet country place. Bedtime is ten unless there's work to be done. Those who want night-life — gambling and so on — can go to such places. . . ."

Howard was foolish enough to say that at Slipton there was no casino.

" No, indeed," said my father, " then you had better sail your punt to Cannes or Monte Carlo. We want none of these imported, Continental ways."

The allusion to Miss Letterby was too direct and too fierce to be missed, or by Howard, in his mood of desperate chivalry, to be passed over. He flushed hotly, squared his shoulders and was about to reply, when Ann intervened :

" I think it would be quite a harmless expedition, Father. The evenings are warm and we should be back early."

" Unchaperoned ? And how do you propose to get

back at all — trapesing up from Slipton in the dark ? ”

“ Mr. Featherford has a motor-car.”

“ May be,” said my father, “ but in my opinion it’s not good enough. A bunch of young people, not too steady some of them, going off——”

“ Do you mean,” Howard inquired icily, “ that all river picnics are wrong ? ”

“ I mean that I’m not in the box to be cross-examined by you. I have said no, and I mean no, and there’s an end of it. What you do personally is your own concern, though I always supposed you had more sense. But there it is,” my father continued with quiet, stifling anger, his eyes alight and his fingers plucking at the crease of the table-cloth, “ I’ve known other men than you make fools of themselves and throw their lives away. But none, I will say, abler than you.” A long bitter pause followed. A servant had come into the room and we waited, in the scent of apple-peel, until she was gone. “ None abler,” my father continued. “ Still, go your own way. But Ann stays here. . . . David, too, for that matter.”

Ann, who was on his right, reached across the corner of the table and laid her hand on his. It was an unprecedented gesture ; for, except to say good-night, we never touched one another.

“ Aren’t ‘ six days enough to quarrel in ’ ? ” she said.

It had been, we all knew, my mother’s phrase, and Ann’s use of it now had effect. The deep creases in my father’s face puckered, he turned his hand over and for a moment shut his fingers upon hers, then pushed back his chair.

“ Very well. Say no more.”

Later, sitting beside Howard’s chair in the garden,

I asked him : " Does that mean, do you think, that the river picnic is on or off ? "

" Ann was wise enough not to ask. She has more sense in her little finger than . . ." As he let the sentence drift away unfinished, I waited until he said : " He couldn't have climbed down then, but if we say no more — you'll see."

Soon he shut the book he had brought out to read and strolled into the house. He was on his way to the Manor. Though he did not come in to tea, no one asked where he was.

" Do you really want to go on this — this expedition ? " my father asked.

" Yes," Ann said, " I should like to."

" That surprises me. That is what——"

" Oh no, I think the river——"

" You mean," my father said denyingly and with protective warning in his voice, " that you'll enjoy it in that company ? "

" I want to go," Ann said. " David and I will keep each other company."

" Very well," my father said, " you know your own business. But you must ask Mrs. Seaford to go with you of course, and tell me she has agreed."

Ann did not argue. " I am sure she will agree," she said.

After tea, she and I sat in the garden together, propped against a grassy bank in the sun. It was long since I had talked quietly with her ; now for a little while at least — perhaps because we were both tired of our separate buffetings — it was possible again. There was a heap of mown grass near at hand ; I let it run through my fingers and smelt them, and wondered,

I don't know why, whether at that moment Rose's squirrel was in or out of its cage. All the time, Ann and I were talking in our own tentative way, with gaps of silence in which the lime shadows grew measurably longer, and yet our talk seemed to us consecutive. It was a kind of thinking-aloud together. Now, for the sake of calm, she had gone below the surface of her own rough sea, and, since we were talking of miracles, drew me into telling her again the story of Baucis and Philemon at whose door the gods came knocking in disguise.

" It always seems odd to me," I said, " that no one believes in *those* gods any more. I don't see how it stopped. Of course, Euripides was a sceptic — anyhow Mr. Letterby says he was — but Mr. Letterby says you can't really be sceptical about a thing unless you believe in it."

" That sounds too clever for me."

" Oh no," I exclaimed, " I see what he means."

" What does he mean ? "

" Well," I said, " I was thinking about it, and it seems to me that if Baucis and Philemon had been sceptics, of course they wouldn't have *recognized* the gods, but if they had been — well, I mean, if they had been people who never thought of the gods at all, then there wouldn't have been any knock at their door."

" I wonder," Ann said. The shadow grew a yard. " Do you ever feel, David, quite sure that something's going to happen before it happens, and yet——"

" Yet what ? "

" You don't know beforehand what the ' something ' is."

I shook my head. " I don't see . . . If——"

" Oh yes ! " she said, " it does make sense, really. You don't know what the thing is, but — but you hear it coming and you know you will recognize it when it comes."

" Like a poem ? " I said.

" A poem ? "

" Or I suppose," I said, " it's perfectly possible that Baucis and Philemon may have heard the travellers' footsteps a long way off. He looked at her and said : Do you hear that ? She nodded and said : I thought I heard something. And then they listened and decided it was nothing after all, but when the knock *did* come——"

" Is that in the story ? "

I was bound to admit that Ovid hadn't said so. But it sounded right to me.

" To me, too," Ann replied, turning over on the grass.

Her confidence gave me boldness. " Ann, why do you think Father behaved like that ? "

" He wanted to help."

" Wasn't that right ? "

She said nothing but lay there quietly, her chin supported by her hands, and I remembered that when Telemachus, who had always seemed to me a timorous creature, had said to his father that there were tens and tens of suitors and that they had better not move against them until they had gathered allies, Odysseus had asked him whether he thought that Athene and Zeus were enough or whether they should look for some other champion. Ann felt — perhaps she knew — that the gods were on her side.

Howard came home to supper, bright-eyed, care-worn, studiously calm. We were in the drawing-room then. My father had not yet come down.

" You must get Mrs. Seaford to come," Ann said. " If you do, it's all settled."

" Listen, Ann. If you hate this, I'll call it off. I'll call it all off. I'll——"

" I think that would be foolish," Ann said, " if Rose has set her heart on it."

22

Except to those who will be exempt barbarians to the end, moments of enlightenment or of disillusion come, in which it is observed that something exists in the affairs of men that is neither funny nor absurd nor at all comfortable, something wry rather than hilarious and yet irresistible, which in self-protection we call comedy. Hitherto, in our salad days, we have supposed comedy to be a joke; if we never grow up, we continue in that belief, braying happily at the incongruous when we see it, without compassion for Malvolio's cross-garters; but if we mature a little before we die, it enters our minds at some time or other that this flavour of comedy is extremely pervasive, like that of lemon, affecting the sour as well as the sweet. Is it not our disproportion against the sunset, our echo in the cave? Is it not a sense of vanity in all things which prevents delight from cloying and tragedy from drugging the soul?

I was far from having reached this formidable conclusion on the evening of the river picnic, but there were moments when this taste was on my lips, giving to sensation a new sharpness. I suffered and I adored; I was deeply troubled because those I loved were suffering and everything was a little out of tune. I was awed by the enchantments of the hour and of my own senses, and yet to the solemn music I was playing to myself there were now and then disconcerting and, if the truth be told, enlivening echoes.

As this was to be a grown-up party, to which I went not as a supplementary child but in my own right, it was important that I should be correctly dressed. Howard was the model to be followed. Not shorts but long white trousers were necessary, and I persuaded the housemaid to iron them. A tennis-shirt was for me more difficult; my habit was to wear it open; but Howard was wearing a bow-tie, and the problem could not be solved until he had lent me one and secured it adroitly in a way that covered the gap. While I stood with my chin up and he, on the edge of the bed, performed this ceremony, I said: " If she sees the gap anyway and the tie comes up all round my neck, it will be worse than wearing the shirt open."

" If who sees it ? "

" Rose."

" Damn Rose and all women ! " he said. " I don't dress to please them. I dress to please myself. . . . Of course, you must wear a tie."

" Why ? "

" Because it's the sort of party at which one does."

So I stood with my chin up, wondering why, and afterwards put new laces in my tennis-shoes and did my hair again with Howard's mixture called Honey and Flowers — all with the same delighted sense of ceremony and of escape from the humdrum which I had had once when being dressed to play the part of Wall in private theatricals — but now I had asked " why ? " and had known that when Howard cursed Rose and all women and tugged fiercely at my bow he was bewitched. I washed my hands and face for the third time and, through my towel, shouted the lines of my part in *A Midsummer-Night's Dream* :

> " *In this same interlude it doth befall*
> *That I, one Snout by name, present a wall. . . .*"

" What are you mumbling about ? " cried Howard from the next room and thrust his head in through the open doorway. " Now you'll have to do your hair again."

" Does Matho come here for us first or go to the Manor ? "

" Here. There's Ann's hamper to put on board. Besides," Howard added, " if Featherford went to the Manor first, it's ten to one Rose wouldn't turn up at Slipton at all."

" Seriously ? But the party was her idea."

Howard, speaking out of his agitation, had said more than he intended ; now he went on : " I know it was. But it isn't any more, because Mrs. Seaford's coming. Anyhow, she pretends that's the reason ; she says Mrs. S. will spoil it all. Of course, she knows that's nonsense. Still there's no arguing with her. If I try, she makes a face and says she isn't the Lord Chancellor, and won't listen, and behaves like a spoilt child, and then . . . the next minute it's all over . . . and she — oh, but she's mad," Howard exclaimed, " it's like trying to harness a bee."

" And yet," I said gravely, " she can be quite serious."

Howard looked up at me — he was lacing his shoes — with the expression of a man in a net. " I know, I know, I know. That's what makes her such hell."

Matho's car arrived and announced itself by hooting.

Because I was of solitary habit and for so long had been ridden by the anxieties of my examination now less than four weeks ahead, the noise of that horn filled me with a sense of festivity. I wasn't excluded, after all! I was one of the crowd, and to prove it I began to shout down to Matho from the window and was not checked even by the discovery behind him of his bony, brown-eyed sister.

" Go down," said Howard, " and help carry the hamper out."

I began to whirl out of the room but went more sedately when I remembered how well I was dressed and how insecure was my tie. In the hall, I found Ann, seated on a great basket. She came to life at sight of me, but not before I had been struck by the forlornness of her attitude in repose. My elation ebbed away. Everything that for a moment I had forgotten — that Howard was betraying her, that Rose was her enemy (my thought chose the harsh, the melodramatic words) and that life, my own life too, had become inextricably confused and entangled — flowed in on a tide of melancholy. Outside, Matho's cheerful hooting became an assault. Ann's summery clothes and my own carefully smoothed hair became a mockery. I hated the party and was suddenly afraid when Howard's footsteps creaked on the stairs behind me. Ann's face was lifted towards him; her eyes travelled beyond me with the expression of one waiting to be recognized; and I knew, from her turning away of her head, that once more Howard had avoided her eyes.

On the way to the Manor we scarcely spoke. Rose was waiting on the steps, her hair in the distance a golden haze, a huge straw hat slung like a shield on her arm. She gave it to me as she climbed in, and I held it on my knees vertically, the scent of the straw in my nostrils, hardly able to see over its edge. If she was, as Howard had feared, in ill-humour with the party, she gave no sign of it. Silence ended with her coming. Everyone began to talk at once or, rather, to shout against the roar of the engines. I alone was silent, not gloomily now, for I was abruptly launched into excitement, but because I was lost in the wild inconsequence of it all and could find nothing on earth to say. This was to be unequal to the occasion ; this was to be a shy schoolboy. I opened my mouth to speak half a dozen times but everything I could think of was too serious. My courage failed me. Everyone, I thought, would notice that I was taking no part, and the dreadful moment would fall in which someone would say : " Well, David, you're very silent." In the hope of warding this off, I was taking refuge behind Rose's hat, when Miss Featherford astonishingly spoke.

My mind at that moment was plunged in the knowledge that Howard had trembled when Rose took her place beside him ; he was now turned away from her and talking to Ann very fast, as though he were grasping and snatching at something that came away in his hand. The words " he is drowning " had formed themselves in my mind, and I was saying to myself " drowning . . . drowning " in time with the throb of the car, when a deep brown voice beside me asked whether I was fond of strawberries, and I saw that Miss Featherford was wearing a huge garnet-ring on her right hand. The garnet recurs much later on the gunwale of another punt sliding past our own, and again at supper. With that Miss Featherford vanishes, to become, I believe, an ambassadress.

Nevertheless I still recall my grateful feeling towards her. She was precisely the kind of woman — girl, I suppose, by the counting of years — who has always paralysed me. Gruff, cheerful, slangy, a gusty talker about dead birds, dying fish and alive horses, she seemed to wear leather where others of her sex wore ribbons. I was not even shy of her, so remote from me did she seem, and had been completely unaware that she was beside me. I assumed that we were as far apart as an Eskimo from a Hottentot and that communication between us was impossible in the nature of things. For all the initiative I should have taken, we might have been silent through eternity on a desert island. No doubt she was as little interested in me. But she troubled to ask whether I liked strawberries and whether I didn't prefer horses to motor-cars, and listened to a reply inevitably voluble and almost certainly, before it was done, Hellenic. She had breeding and suffered fools officially, as an ambassadress should; and she was kind. Of such, when the gods play the game, are the kingdoms of this world.

At Slipton, Tony Seaford and I avoided each other. Each of us was determined that we should not be paired off together as schoolboys. On the rickety landing-stage, we said hello and parted, to busy ourselves in aloof detachment with hampers and cushions, and were careful not to recognize each other again until we could make signals from separate punts.

Certain aspects and moments of that river picnic come back to me with rare intensity but the structure of it is lost. Though I am sure I could not punt, I must have been encouraged to try, for I can feel one particular thrust when the pole gripped a pebbly bottom at the right depth, just as it should, and came away cleanly, and the punt sprang forward with a chuckle and a gliding throb.

" Straight as a die ! " said Matho from under my feet, and Rose, looking up from the bows with Howard stretched out beside her, clapped her hands.

When Howard was punting, Matho, I expect, took his place, but once at least it was I who lay at her side.

" Look," she said, pointing at Matho, " he's asleep."

Indeed he was, curled up neatly like a great dog on a hearth.

" But why ? " I said.

" Well," she answered, " he went to the Derby on Wednesday and stayed for the Oaks. And now he's recovering from his winnings."

She sat up in her place with her finger to her lips, and leaning forward gazed at him long and curiously. Howard was prepared to drop water on him from the punt-pole, but she waved it away, and lowered herself again on to our cushions.

" Napoleon," I said in a whisper with no other intent than to laugh at Matho, " slept during the battle of Jena."

" And won it," she whispered back.

How quiet it was ! One of the other punts, with Tony and Marjorie Seaford and my ambassadress in it, was extricating itself from overhanging willows on the farther side of our bend ; the third had fallen behind. Howard was driving us forward so gently and smoothly that there was never a swerve or a jolt. We were in that fortnight before midsummer when the year is still.

Nothing is urgent. The thrust of spring and the retreats of autumn are far enough away; the season tells for a few days of nothing but itself, poised between memory and presage. Time loiters; the grass lies with open blade, a pliant greenness with unwrinkled edge. Seen through shallow water, when I looked over the edge of the punt, brown and blue pebbles had a gleam as crisp as the sound of bells on a frosty day, and when I leaned back again and gazed up at the empty, cooling sky, I forgot men and was happy.

It puzzled me that the Greek gods should have bothered themselves about us so persistently. Why, for example, did the three goddesses submit their dispute to the shepherd of Mount Ida? They knew quite well what it would lead to: a long war, to say nothing of the homeward journey of Odysseus, in which they would have to intervene again and again. Why didn't they stay in their own world, at most driving chariots about the sky, and not get mixed up with ours?

There were two possible answers: either that it amused them, or that they couldn't help it, and were themselves subject to other gods who played with them. Perhaps both answers were true.

" Say something," said Rose. " If you had three wishes, what would you wish? "

" To get my scholarship and—" My wishes bumped against that huge rock. " Really," I said, " it's much more exciting to see it the other way round."

She turned her head inquiringly.

" I mean," I continued, " everyone sees himself as the person a god comes to and says: what do you wish? The really exciting thing is: if you were a god, what would you do? "

" I see," Rose answered, " the other end of the wand. . . . I know what I should do : I should make myself invisible and go everywhere, and when Matho woke up he should be a horse and—" She broke off suddenly. " No," she said, " what I should really do is — is remake myself from the beginning so that somehow I was all one through and through, so that I didn't feel half-false whatever I did."

" But you aren't false now," I said piously.

" Why not ? "

" Because when you say you want to remake yourself——"

" Oh, pooh! " she said, " that's because you expect so much of me. It doesn't stop me wanting to turn Howard into — into — oh, you know your Shakespeare ! — ' the triple pillar of the world trans-formed——' "

But I didn't know. *Antony and Cleopatra* was a play I hadn't read. My shame in not knowing preserves the words over forty years : " the triple pillar of the world transformed into a strumpet's fool ".

" Oh, well," she said, marking my silence, " thank God for that. . . . Put it this way, then. All my noble sentiments don't prevent my wanting to turn Matho into a horse and ride him with spurs. Is that enough ? Is it ? Look at him. . . . No, don't look ! "

She pulled up her huge hat from where it was lying across her knees and covered both our faces with it. Her breathing lifted its brim ; and how fast she was breathing ! Light, penetrating the straw, drew needle-points and thin lines upon her cheeks, as though a net of gold were spread over them. Within the tent were all the perfumes of Arabia. But when she opened her

eyes and looked at me through the net, some devil of
comedy gave me the wit to understand that she was
watching only my likeness to Howard. She let the hat
fall away and turned over with her back to me. If I had
been Howard, she would have taken me in her arms.

The punt, under his faultless guidance, had been
turned into the little inlet where we were all to meet
for supper. As it rubbed against the bank, Matho and
Rose sat up and stared at each other, she smiling at his
lazily bewildered air.

"Good-morning," he said at last, "is it a fine
day?" and she burst out laughing, for he was rubbing
his eyes and stretching himself, and this was the kind
of acted joke that she enjoyed.

At supper I fell into conversation with Matho. He
told me of the Derby and the Oaks, and I was flattered
by the ease with which he disregarded my ignorance.
Meanwhile, among the chinking of glasses and the
popping of bottles, Howard dominated the conversation
so powerfully that I wished, for his sake, he had known
how to play. With Mrs. Seaford he was charming.
She had the half-timid stateliness of an elderly lady
who had once been the sweet foolishness of such parties
as this, and he knew how to make her feel that she was
welcome for her own sake and that her former prettiness
was remembered. He made Miss Featherford laugh
by telling her a story, invented on the spur of the
moment, about her garnet-ring: she did not follow
the story, but she caught at phrases in it and repeated
them with loud exclamations like the report of salute
guns, and felt that, plain though she might be, she
was not being neglected. Indeed, as long as Howard
troubled to make her so, she was the centre of attention;

as long as he could tell a story or discourse on some subject — any subject, for he could be gay as well as serious — he shone ; nor did he fail in the give-and-take of conversation ; but it had to be conversation with a thread, not chirruping at random, and he had to shine.

Rose was gently taunting Matho for having gone to sleep.

" And now you shall tell us what you were dreaming about."

" You," he said at random.

" That's not true. You mustn't make things up. What were you really dreaming about ? "

And Matho, who knew his musical comedies, broke into song :

> " *When you and I*
> *Are parted by*
> *Three thousand miles of sea. . . .*"

" Presumably," Howard said, " the Atlantic."

Matho continued unperturbed, strumming an imaginary guitar and periodically making cheerful noises to indicate an orchestral accompaniment :

> " *When you and I*
> *Are parted by*
> *Three thousand miles of sea,* (Ting-a-ling)
> *I wonder : shall I dream of you,*
> *And will you dream of me ?* (Tong-a-long)
> *For if you don't and I do do,*
> *When shades of evening fall,*
> *I'd very much rather stay here with you*
> *And not go to sleep at all —*
> (Tong, tong ; tong tinkety tong)
> *And not go to sleep at all.*

A Breeze of Morning

(Chorus! Chorus!)
Dancing, dreaming,
Give me your answer, do:
Shall I dream all day
Long miles away
Or dance all night with you?'

I moved my mouth so that everyone might suppose
me to be joining in the chorus. When the voices
raggedly ceased, Rose, who perhaps found relief from
personal stress in the rollicking inanity of Matho's
performance, applauded like a child, looking at Howard
almost piteously as if to say: Applaud too! Keep it
up! It makes everything easier! But Howard began
to analyse the song mercilessly and amusingly, as
though it were a fragment of papyrus which provided
the only surviving evidence of a buried civilization.
Why was the man in question going away? Had he
quarrelled with the lady? Was the all-night dance
some kind of ritual performance? A picture of
mysterious barbarism emerged, with Matho in the
foreground as the principal savage. It was an adroit
piece of satirical nonsense which had us smilingly
expectant, and Matho, being appealed to at the end
of it, fell into Howard's trap, and began to sing the
song again. But the bubble had been pricked. This
time the song dragged. Even the chorus was half-
hearted:

" *Dancing, dreaming,*
Give me your answer, do:
Shall I dream all day
Long miles away
Or . . ."

Poor Matho's voice died away on his failure, and Howard, in the triumph of his cleverness, went too far.

" I'm inclined to think," he said, " that, at law, the demand for an answer amounts, in the context, to a proposal of marriage."

Instantly Rose flamed at him, as a child might at someone who had burst her balloon. Her anger was as excessive as his provocation of it had been unwise. In other company, in different circumstances, his dry fooling would have pleased. She was tormented by it. It left her behind. Her flush was the flush of humiliation. " I think you're horrible ! " she exclaimed. " Yes, horrible and cruel. . . . I think it was a good song. And we were all enjoying ourselves, weren't we ? "

He was confounded but answered with icy self-control : " My dear Rose, I hadn't a notion that I was being cruel to anyone."

" That's just the trouble. You never have."

" To whom was I being cruel ? "

" Everyone. No one. Oh, I don't know, and I don't care."

" Well," said Howard with calmness worse than a shout, " in any case, I apologize. And I'm sorry if I have been boring, and——"

" Boring ! " she exclaimed with extraordinary vehemence. " You aren't that. Sometimes I wish to heaven you were."

There were tears in her voice.

Howard reached out for his glass. " All right," he said, turning to Matho, " then I apologize to you."

" My dear chap, that's all right. All's fair in —

well, anyhow, tell you the truth, I haven't an idea what it's all about. Seldom have with you. . . . Least said the better, if you ask me."

We took his advice. Through all this, Ann had said nothing. Now, to ease away silence, she began to talk to Mrs. Seaford. We joined in eagerly and handed out more food and drink. Rose with a jug in her hand, which she refused to let Henry Seaford take from her, came round to fill everyone's glass and Howard's last. She sat beside him.

"I'm sorry," I heard her say, and when he had murmured an answer: "It's no good, you know."

"What isn't?"

"Us."

I suppose they were beyond caring whether I heard or not. A clatter of forks killed his reply.

"Oh, Howard," she pleaded, "do be nice!"

"'Nice?' . . . My darling, I——"

"Easy. . . . Slack . . . I don't know. . . . Just for this evening, couldn't you?"

If they had been able then to separate and let time pass, they might have been healed, but a river party is unrelenting. Supper jangled, the repacking of the baskets was an exercise in politeness and good temper, we were glad to get into our punts again; but that part of the evening which should have been the pleasantest lay ahead in time and no one would admit failure by abandoning it, no one would say: let us go home.

Matho avoided our punt. In the reshuffle Tony Seaford took his place.

"If you punt like that," Rose said to Howard, "we shall be back at Slipton an hour too soon."

So we tied up to the bank and talked in the eye of the sunset. It was peaceful enough. The quarrel was far away, but life had gone with it. I thought of the work I had left undone that day and of my bedroom at home with its accusing books. When I get back, I wildly promised myself, I will work all night, and, although I knew well that I should fall asleep, I imagined myself propped with sufficient discomfort on my elbow. But no sooner had the blessed inclusion of books taken possession of me than I remembered the door communicating between Howard's room and mine, and wondered: what shall we say? shall we part, and shut the door, and go to bed silently? By then the evening would be over, its opportunities irrecoverable, and it came to me suddenly, like the first shudder of a fever, that by staying where I was, chattering of nothing to Tony Seaford, I was standing like a dolt across the whole course of Howard's life. With what excuse I don't know, I clambered ashore, taking Tony with me. We wandered aimlessly.

" Oh, I say," said Tony, " I'm sick of this. I vote we go back."

But I held him until I heard a shouting of our names.

Howard was already in the bows, fumbling with the painter by which we were tied up. It was difficult to handle in the black shadow of the branches.

" Jump in," he said. " It's early yet, but we may as well go back."

He spoke kindly, as though my coming were a relief. They had, I suppose, reached that condition in which conciliatory words have all been said, and no others will come because now they are a language that has stiffened like a dead face.

Howard punted us down river. Rose lay back against her cushions, saying nothing, almost invisible.

" Ugh ! " she said at last, " I'm cold. Aren't you all shivering ? . . . That beastly hat ! "

She lowered it over the side with calm deliberation as though she had been putting it down on a table. I caught it as it floated past.

" Let it go," she said.

Careful for property, distrustful of feminine whim, I looked up at Howard for orders.

" Let it go," he said.

In spite of the little holes through which the sun had fallen on us, it did not sink at once.

PART THREE

ROSE LETTERBY

23

Coming home from school one afternoon, I entered Letterby Park by the main gate. My intention was to walk across the face of the house, enter by the side-door, see if the Squire was in his room, and, if not, either settle down in what I now regarded as my own card-room or go home by the dingle.

As I emerged from the avenue, I heard the sound of hooves and wheels behind me. A heavy, closed carriage rolled lumberingly past. Once or twice, in bad weather, I had seen it at church, and now and then had met it driving empty about the lanes to exercise the horses. But it was used so rarely that to be over-taken by it on a week-day and to observe two black figures within made me hold my breath. It must have been a very old carriage, with its curling springs, its step at the back, and a dome-like roof of four panels surmounted by a small knob, or effigy of some kind, perhaps the heraldic lion.

It drew up at the steps. Rose and her father got out. She had, perhaps, been negligent in her own family-mourning; if so, it was a negligence that I had not noticed, but she must, I think, have been guilty of it, for certainly the depth, the luxuriance — there is no other word — of the black she was now wearing was a shock to me. It gave her height and made her face small, pale and luminous. The princess in my

tower had become an empress — or a nun. Her
father, as I gazed, caught sight of me, and raised a
summoning ebony stick. He was wearing or, more
accurately, was wrapped in a carefully buttoned frock-
coat, cut high and of astonishing length. A survival
of a vanished dandyism, it had now a columnar effect
which his silk hat continued skyward.

" This young man," he said in a voice that surprised
me by being his ordinary voice, though perhaps more
cheerful than usual, " has a habit of turning up at the
right time. After a funeral the Latin poets are an
admirable corrective. But we'll take a cup of tea first."
He looked at his daughter with momentary hesitation.
Perhaps something in her appearance, or some companionship that had arisen between them during their
drive, touched his heart. "You come and have tea
with us. You don't want to be moping up there in your
own room, I'll be bound. Will you come?"

" Do you mean it? "

" Of course I do. Why not? But I don't want to
drag you. You are your own mistress. Would you
like it? "

" You know I should," she answered.

Hitherto I had always believed that the separateness
of these two lives at the Manor was a result of Rose's
independence, even of her disliking her father. Her
parents had not got on together; she had sided with
her mother: this had been my too simple explanation.
Now she said " You know I should " with a simplicity,
a tentative hopefulness, which opened my eyes. Loneliness I understood; to be separated from one's roots
was a terror I could share; and I remember the
strange contradiction of my feeling, as I heard her

voice, that she was so young as to be within the range of my compassion, and of my seeing, as I looked into her face, the impassable years lying between us.

Rapp, who was standing by the open door, was told to bring tea, and I followed Mr. Letterby along the passage hung with sporting prints. Someone had taken the chance of his absence to clean, though not to tidy, his room. His piles of books and papers remained, but they had been lifted, there was a gloss on the bare patches of table, scraps of colour came up from the carpet, the hearth was swept, the mantelshelf re-ordered, and things that had toppled on to their sides were now on their ends again.

"There appears," he said, "to have been an invasion."

His affability threw me a little out of my stride and I had difficulty in removing from my face and voice that expression of muffled awe which I considered appropriate to funerals. Mr. Letterby would have none of it. He took off his frock-coat, undid the top button of his trousers, and took a familiar Paisley dressing-gown out of a cupboard.

"A long drive," he said, "but thank heaven the carriage is a roomy one; you can stretch your legs. . . . Don't suppose you've noticed it, but funerals make one hungry, so I've found. . . . Besides, he'd had his innings and made the most of it, according to his lights. Still, poor chap, I don't suppose he wanted to go. Who does?"

"Who was he?" I ventured to ask.

"Uncle of Rose's."

The tone in which he said this was so evidently a repudiation of blood relationship that I sheered away from the subject. Anything concerned with family was dangerous ground with Mr. Letterby, and it was not until Rose had joined us and was pouring out tea that he returned to it with a glancing reference of which I did not then take the meaning.

"I told Rapp to put your hat away, Father. It looked too funereal standing there in the hall."

"It has gone to weddings enough, my dear. A cheerful hat in its day before I withdrew from all that kind of thing. . . . I wonder a bit now whether it was worth while."

"What? Withdrawing?"

He shrugged his shoulders. "Oh," he said, "one does what one wants to do, and then invents heroic motives later. Not to wander about Paris and the Riviera was no real sacrifice to me, nor even the stables. There was always half of me wanted to shut myself up. . . . Still what I told myself was that I could save this place, taxation or no taxation, debts or no debts, if I stayed quiet and hung on. So I could have. I've turned the corner. But I needed time. Another five years — ten maybe. Now I shan't get them. After this—" and he made a gesture at the black dress she was wearing — "they'll have to press. Pack of lawyers. I don't blame them."

"This" I understood to be the funeral. Who was to "press" or what they would press for, I did not know, but it was clear to me that something untoward had happened and that Mr. Letterby's unexpected breeziness was his way of meeting it. This impression was strengthened by my noticing that Rose answered as if she were sorry for him and wished, without being sure how she would be received, to be of help.

164

" Probably," she said, " you won't believe it, but I too should be sorry to go."

" Why shouldn't I believe it? It's yours, isn't it? Will be." He drew breath and looked round the room. " Or would have been."

" Yes, but you see, it isn't just that. I'm fond of it. You don't believe me."

He turned up the toes of his neat boots and looked at them with surprise as if they didn't belong to his feet.

" You've said often enough it's boring."

" Perhaps, but one can be fond of boring things if they've been boring long enough and are old enough."

" Chance for me," he said.

The way in which he spoke those last words and looked at her, as he spoke them, with tenderness and yet with a wry, doubtful humour that hedged his risk; the irony, almost the flippancy of tone, with which Rose, offering alliance, safeguarded her approach from sentimentality and so from rebuff; created between them an intentness which I felt without then being able to distinguish its nature. Their cold divisions had always troubled me; my closeness to Ann, my reserved but deep relationship with my father, the seemingly natural unity of my own home, had made the estrangement of the Letterbys appear perverse. Now weren't they quite obviously trying to " make it up "? Why couldn't they?

" Chance for me," Mr. Letterby said.

" Every chance," she replied in a low voice; but added at once, lest she should emotionally overstep the boundary of half-bantering politeness laid down between them: " But it works the other way, doesn't it? "

" Which means ? "

" The old house may be bored with me."

That in speaking of the house she was speaking of him also, he must have known — even I know it now — but he chose, or perhaps by his nature was compelled, to disregard it. He too kept on his side of the boundary. Hunching his shoulders, he began to take off the surprising boots.

Such had been the intentness of their conversation up to this point that, without embarrassing me, it had enabled them to behave, for a minute or two, quite simply as if I had not been there. Their release was to discover me, to give me more to eat and drink, and to forget their own failure.

And yet, something had been accomplished. When the Squire and I began work, Rose said : " Then I must go, I suppose."

" Not," said her father, " if you are disinclined."

The evening was cool. She lighted a fire of wood and lay on the sofa while we worked, not herself reading, not interrupting, glad of his companionship, perhaps of mine. He was old enough and I young enough to give her rest.

24

ROSE in her black dress on her father's sofa, her eyes wide open and staring through our incomprehensible Latin, emerges, as one among two or three clearly defined pictures, from the confused memories of those June days that followed the river picnic. For the rest, I have the feel, rather than an ordered recollection, of that time.

Another clear picture — but this, I think, is an epitome of many — is of Howard, half-undressed, walking up and down my room after I was in bed, and talking, ostensibly to me, in truth to himself. He was telling me urgently, as though I had denied it, that, if he gave up the Bar and went into business — and he described a friend who, he thought, would " give him an opening to-morrow morning " — he could earn money more quickly; and I knew, even while he was speaking, that he didn't believe in the " opening " and, what was more, had no intention of giving up the Bar. He was, it is true, making plans in accordance with his habit, but now there was an element of the irrational in his planning; his intelligence would miss a beat, the argument he had begun drop out of his mind, and he go off on a new scent.

The river picnic was seldom absent from his thought for long. Sometimes he blamed and sometimes justified himself, saying he had " misjudged " his audience or that Rose had behaved like a pettish child, but more often he was puzzled by what had happened and tried again and again to explain it.

"But, Howard," I said, "you made it up with her."

"Oh yes."

"Well then, isn't she all right now?"

Then he lied. "I scarcely see her." Then he forgot that he had lied or that he was speaking to me, and said: "She's like quicksilver . . . or she's like a rag doll." Then, seeing me, he sat down on my bed, and added in his ordinary voice: "The one really unlivable thing is muddle, or so it seems to me, and that river picnic was a muddle. I mean: we were all saying much more — and much less — than we meant. The English usually say much less; when they begin to say much more *at the same time*, then there's hell to pay."

This was typical of Howard: the use of generalizations, each one of which had for him a special and personal meaning; the attempt to explain intellectually a passionate confusion that had swept him away from reason; and, through it all, a patient struggle for lucidity.

Then he took, as it were, another note for the summing-up he was determined to deliver on his own case:

"When you reach a point at which there's no clear right and wrong . . . oh, well," he said, "leave right and wrong out of it. . . . When you reach a point at which parts of your own will are in conflict, and any choice you make unchooses itself again, then — then what's to be done?"

"Sleep," I said.

" Sleep ! That sounds easy ! "

" I don't mean just sleep in bed," I explained.

" Then what on earth do you mean ? "

I couldn't tell him what I meant ; I had spoken half-childishly the first word that had come into my head ; now, though I knew it had been the right word — for " sleep " also means sinking out of the opposed currents and the froth of time, and waiting — I looked at him stupidly and did not answer.

" No," he said, fortifying himself, " the only thing to do is to make up your mind and take all the consequences, one way or the other."

And then, before my eyes, his choice unchose itself, and he rationalized that also.

" And yet," he said, " if you look at history, nine times out of ten the men who have come through are those who had the staying-power to let muddle go on and on and on, and not force the issue until — until it wasn't an issue any more."

" Caesar," I said, " burned his boats."

And Howard, with something of his old spirit, had the grace to answer : " I wonder. . . . Caesar was no fool."

He rose and moved off towards his own room. " Well, I'll take your advice, or try to," and he began yawning. " How's your work, David ? "

My work, looking up at me suddenly out of the confusion into which life had fallen, surprised me by its distance and secrecy. I hadn't the heart to talk of it, but I managed to say : " Oh, all right."

" You're lucky."

" Isn't yours ? "

" My work ? It gets done."

How do we human beings communicate at all, so inadequate is our speech, so deeply buried are its undertones? His life, as he had imagined it, was cracking under him, but he couldn't escape from a kind of measured futility in the words he used. I too sat tight within my convention. Our only reaching out, our only acknowledgement of understanding or affection, was in our inquiries for each other's work, and yet we were drawn together. Though I understood what was happening to the extent of knowing that he was moving to an extreme, my love of Ann did not vitiate my love of him. This faculty of not sitting in judgement belongs, perhaps, only to the very young and the very old. Besides, one fights for one's own absolute needs. Mine was for a coherent world.

" Why," I asked, " don't you do your exercises any more ? "

" Why should I ? "

" You always did."

" Is that a good reason ? "

I sat up in bed, intending to say: " Couldn't we, somehow, all be peaceful again ? " but, if I had said it, he would have thought that I was a little boy, so I lay down again and said nothing.

25

THE third of my vivid recollections marking that period of suspense is of my sister's frightened and distracted face.

It was Saturday, for Howard had not gone to London. Probably he was at the Manor for the greater part of the day: certainly he was there in the afternoon, for, as I approached, I saw him waiting on the side-lawn, and Rose, in a light dress and carrying a basket, join him and walk away at his side. Much later, as I was passing through the hall, I heard them in the gallery above me.

"Oh, Howard," she said, "we have been over all that again and again and again."

"Still," he answered, "we haven't got it clear, and we must. Our whole lives depend on it."

"I'm not sure they do."

"What do you mean?"

"I don't know what I mean. I'm tired, that's all. If we were capable of going mad, shouldn't we have gone mad by now?"

The sitting-room door shut. The gallery was empty and the hall so quiet that a bluebottle, swinging up into the slack air and angrily swerving and plunging, made a tearing sound, which dimly reverberated, like that of a string breaking within a shut violin-case.

I had been on the way back to the card-room,

intending to work for another hour before going home. The *Odyssey* was lying open near the end of the tenth book, at the point where the Squire and I had left it, and I stared at the open page without sitting down; but I was not thinking of how Odysseus left the isle of Aeaea or of poor Elpenor who, in the haste of departure, fell off the roof and broke his neck; for, though my eyes read of these things, I was thinking of the last words I had heard from the gallery and repeating them to myself. When she said, " If we had been capable of going mad," she meant, " If we had it in us to cut adrift, to liberate ourselves " — that I understood well enough; but I was not trying to analyse the conversation I had overheard nor was I asking: what has happened between them? I was listening for echoes.

Certain words, I felt then and feel now, have, or may have, a power independent of their designed meaning. The great legends which have held the imagination of mankind are never empty, and few have held it so firmly as those which tell of words that open doors or summon genii or command the birds of the air. Words are keys: in themselves nothing, until they lock or unlock. They are paths in the wood where we are lost, each in itself no more than a few yards of bracken, until suddenly one path cries out to be followed; we obey, and are in open country. Words are a bundle of dry sticks, but who knows which will blossom in his hand and become a wand?

The words Rose had used gleamed at me like a mysterious shape seen through water. If I could reach so far, it would have value and use that I could not yet distinguish. Seeing before me this shining talisman,

I forgot the words it had represented; the symbol replaced the actuality, which was allowed to sleep. The hot, dusty weariness of the discussion I had over-heard faded away. I began to walk up and down the card-room telling myself stories, and soon found myself in the open air, the *Odyssey* tucked under my arm, my feet speeding homeward, my imagination brimming.

Wasn't there a story to be told of a man who picked up a key on which was written: " Keep me until you have found my lock "? It would not be on a lawn that one would expect to find such a key, but in the rough grass beyond, or leaning against the root of an elm. Breaking my pace, I began to loiter and look about me, and go out of my way to touch the bark of an elm that would not let me pass until I had touched it; and so I was happy until I said to myself that this was a childish proceeding and set off homeward with a business-like tread.

Ann was coming towards me. At first, she was small and her face indistinguishable, for she had only just come out of the dingle. Why was she here? Why was she going to the Manor now? Unease, a sense of the unfamiliar, almost of the unnatural, grew in me, and I halted, a shiver of apprehensiveness running up my spine into my hair; for though she whom I saw was unquestionably Ann, with the same pliancy of body and straight carriage of the head, she had neither Ann's ease nor her detached way of moving leisurely and observantly — indeed she seemed not to be observing at all, she did not glance up at the sky as Ann would have done or turn her head to look at the trees and meadows; she was walking as if she were blind, and not only as if she saw nothing but as if she felt and tasted nothing. The Ann I knew had a worshipping familiarity with natural things, she was constantly alive to the feel, the scent, the sound of them; her habit of life, her way of listening and watching and letting the air run through her fingers, was an acknowledgement and a receiving of them; while the Ann I saw now came on with no movement but a forward movement, in a sheath of disregard.

I waved, but she made no answer. I waved again, and she came on without a sign. I called, and after an interval she turned her head a little, as though she were remembering a sound rather than hearing it, but turned it not towards but away from me. She altered neither pace nor direction.

The path she had chosen was that on which Rose had first offered to give me French lessons. I was on higher ground and to her right. Her face was now visible but not the detail of its expression. There was something wild and lost and driven in the regularity of her advance and in the climb of her shadow before her, step by step, which so differed from my knowledge of her that it cried out in me for explanation, and I said to myself: is she walking in her sleep? Is it possible, in full daylight, that she is walking in her sleep? What had become of my sister? What had become of the natural reason of the world? I saw now that her eyes were open, though they did not see me, and I asked: do sleep-walkers have their eyes open or shut? Open, I thought, and began to run towards her. My lips were open to call her name — I was within thirty yards by now — when I remembered having heard that a sleep-walker must not be awakened violently, so I let her pass by at that distance, standing rooted as though she were a ghost; then followed, rubbing my feet through the grasses with a kind of stealthiness, and, when I had almost overtaken her, compelled myself to speak her name. She went on. Perhaps I had not spoken loudly enough. Though the sunshine and the cawing rooks had become a lock upon silence, I repeated her name; she did not turn; and suddenly I sprang forward and passed her and stood in her way.

" David."

Perhaps I had always known that she was not sleep-walking; one knows and one does not know. Now, looking into her face, the face of one beside herself, walking on and on towards the edge of a cliff, I knew that the tables were turned between us two. It was she who was dependent and in my charge. She was like a lost child, with the fierce, unreasoning deter-mination of a child to strike, to assert itself, to escape from the dreadful enclosure of being lost. She, who had been for me so wise, so old, so invulnerable, so sure, had broken. How her eyes shone! How her lips trembled! How wild she was — with desperate light-nings running through her — faith, patience, judgement, hope, all gone.

" Where are you going ? "

" To the Manor."

" Why ? "

" To see Rose."

" You can't."

" I can."

" No, no, no, no," I said, seizing her arm.

" I must. Oh, David, you're a little boy. You don't understand. Get out of the way."

" Please, please," I said, " don't go now." I kept
fast hold on her arm.

" Is he there ? "

" Yes."

" Oh, David, what am I to do? The lawn was
empty and I couldn't bear it; it had been empty so
long. . . . It was like being buried inside a glass
mountain. . . . If I went to Rose and said . . . That
will end it somehow; somehow that will break the — I
mean, it will break the glass which . . ."

I slid my hand down to her hand. " Ann, let's go
home," and she clutched me and came with me.

Many wise things appeared in my mind that I
wished to say, but I had words for none of them. It
seemed to me that my sister had been drawn out of
her natural self, that she had been under a spell as she
came up from the dingle. If I had not been there . . .
and even now she was walking in a dazed way, silently,
and our silence deepened and stiffened because I hadn't
the words which, if spoken, would break the spell and
restore her to herself again. Tell me what to say, tell
me what to say, I implored the gods again and again,
just as, when the devil rises up in a dream, one searches
for the talismanic words which, if spoken, will beat
him down.

I could find nothing. But when people are un-
happy and there is nothing else to be done, you offer
them as a gift something which, however useless it may
be to them, is precious to you. A child brings its doll,
and a dog its bone. So I began, because to do so was
to establish a customary link between us, to bring Ann
my day's work for her approval, and told her that
Mr. Letterby and I had been finishing the tenth book

of the *Odyssey* — " you know, Ann, the bit where Odysseus decides that he must leave Circe's island and thinks he is going straight home, but is told by the goddess that first he must go down into Hades, and then . . ."

Ann did not speak, but she tightened her hold on me, and I thought she was listening. At any rate I went on, because I had nothing else to say or to give her.

" Odysseus argued about his journey and complained, after weeping and grovelling, that he didn't know his way and had no guide, and the goddess told him—" I paused, discouraged, for Ann was making no response, and, in the pause, an echo came into my mind : if only you had the capacity to go mad, if only you had the capacity to be simple, if only you didn't argue and argue. . . .

" Well," said Ann's voice at my side, " what did she tell him ? "

" Oh," I answered, " quite obviously she thought he argued too much. She told him to get his mast up and hoist sail and *sit down*, and leave it to the breeze to carry his ship where he had to go."

" ' Sit down,' " Ann repeated.

It struck me as odd that she should have repeated those particular words. They were the words Mr. Letterby had hit upon and chuckled over. I told her about it eagerly, for I had her attention at last. " I am always pleased when someone puts Odysseus in his place," Mr. Letterby had said. " Circe never failed. She gave him all his styles and titles and then discreetly snubbed him. ' Son of Laertes, of the seed of Zeus, Odysseus of many devices, trouble not thyself ' — in other words, don't be so infernally clever; the gods will provide, if only you'll let them."

I told my sister this as best I could. " Mr. Letterby said," I added, " that it was like the story of Naaman in the Old Testament. He said that our chief silliness as men was to teach the gods how to do their business."

We were in the dingle by now.

" What made you start for home at this hour ? " Ann asked. " It's early for you."

" I don't know. I didn't mean to. A story came into my head, so I just came out."

" Was it about Odysseus ? "

" No. It was about a key."

" I wonder what made you tell me about him."

I couldn't remember.

" David," she said, as we came out of the dingle into our own garden, " say that piece again."

" Which ? "

" Beginning with the ' styles and titles ' . . ."

An encore is rare in a sleep-walking scene, but I found it nevertheless agreeable. I gave her the opening of Circe's speech, as far as I could remember it, in Greek, then in English :

" Son of Laertes, of the seed of Zeus, Odysseus of many devices, trouble not thyself for a guide but——"

" Bless you," Ann said. " No, let's not go into the house yet. Come and sit on the lawn. Go on telling me your story."

" Well then, of course, they sailed away and came to——"

" I don't mean that story. I mean your own — about the key."

I answered that there was no story except that once

upon a time there was a wood-cutter's son who found a key, propped against the root of an elm. He brought it home proudly and said : " Look what I have found ! " but they all laughed at him and said : " What is the good of a rusty old key ? " So night after night, when his work was done and he came in from the forest, he slept with the key under his pillow——

" Why ? "

" So that no one should steal it. . . . No, I mean : because he didn't want his brothers to see it and laugh at him and throw it away. And then one night, or in the very early morning, he heard the key say from under the pillow, close to his ear : Polish me. But he did nothing——"

" Why ? "

" Because he thought he had been dreaming. And the next night, the key said again : Polish me, and made itself hard under his cheek ; so he took it out and put it under his mattress. The third night — the third night, his mattress felt as though it had a mountain under it as big as Vesuvius. It heaved and rumbled like a volcano, so he dragged it back and threw the key out of the window. ' My brothers were right,' he said to himself, ' what is the good of a rusty old key ? Now I shall be able to sleep.' But in the morning, when he woke up, he found the key in his hand, and it said : ' Polish me '. After that, he took it out into the forest every day, and whenever no one was looking, he polished it. The rust came away little by little. On the seventh day it was all gone, and he was disappointed ; he had expected something marvellous to happen — the key to turn into gold or into — well, anyhow, into something it wasn't — but it was

179

just like any other key, until, as he turned it over and over in his hand, he saw that something was written on it, but it was in Greek, and——"

" Oh no, David, we can't have that ! " said Ann, gloriously laughing at me.

" Why not ? "

" Anyhow, we can't."

" Very well," I said, wishing only to continue my story without interruption, " it was in any language you like, and what it said was : ' Keep me until you find my lock '."

Ann was silent now. I could have gone on without interruption if I had had any more to say, but I hadn't.

" Well ? " she said at last.

" There isn't any more."

" But there must be ! How did it end ? "

" I haven't got there yet."

She made no attempt to force me. " Anyhow," she said, " it's a good story."

" I suppose it depends, really, on what it did unlock," I suggested, half hoping that she might tell me.

" I think *that* depends on who he was," she said. " That's why it's a good story."

26

AT church next morning neither the Squire nor his daughter appeared. Howard was at home all day, silent and avoiding. What had passed between him and Rose I have still no means of knowing. At the time I thought they had quarrelled, for I did not then know that a time may come to lovers who are hot for each other but without confidence, without peace, when to discuss how they may escape and be together becomes a repetitive weariness and even their kisses are no more than a way of silencing themselves.

My father, however observant his eye or bitter his thought, ruled himself not to intervene. He had his absolute loyalties. He had received Howard into our home as one of ourselves and had made no conditions; as long as outwardly the rules were kept, he would impose no conditions that touched Howard's personal life. He had offered security while Howard made his way at the Bar, and, unless Howard by a wild, visible folly deliberately released him, would keep his contract to the uttermost farthing. So I have no doubt his mind worked, for so it worked with regard to us, his children. Whatever the world might do or we might do, he was unchanging. He would never let us down. " There are always," he said once, " good reasons for not keeping one's word. They are all bad." Therefore when Howard stayed at home that Sunday afternoon and was seen making his way into the garden with a brief-case under his arm, my father viewed this unexpected renewal of activity with an ironical smile, but said no more than : " Busier than usual ? "

" A few things to catch up with," Howard answered.

My sister, so fiercely distracted yesterday, was calm again to-day. Never again, after my experience of the rebellious fire in her, did I take her for granted as a background to my own life, but loved her no less deeply because I was enabled to see her now as young, passionate and fallible. Nor did she appear to me the less good for being a little farther from the angels. Her discord of the day before had, I think, been resolved, as discords may often be in music, " by descending one step ". There can be pride even in humility, even in acceptance, and she had been emptied of it. Her faith was no weaker — how shall I say it except in terms of my old legends ? — because it was less exacting of the gods.

As I went through the house on my way to the Manor — Howard being then far away with his brief-case at the other end of the garden — I heard her at her piano through the closed drawing-room door. I paused to listen because the music, in a way I didn't at first understand, was both familiar and unfamiliar. It dawned on me that she was playing *her* part in one of the duets that she and Howard had been accustomed to play together.

Mr. Letterby was not in his room, but I had work enough to occupy me. Before settling down to it, I walked along the front of the house with the intention of staring at the bright red motor-car which I had seen at the steps. I disliked it, but it fascinated me because I thought of it as a horseless chariot and wondered what Achilles would have made of it if it had come out, rumbling and banging, from the walls of Troy.

To my surprise, I found Matho sitting patiently at the wheel.

" Not working ? " he said.

" Mr. Letterby isn't there."

" I'm stranded too. Rose isn't either. . . . Sunday afternoon walk, I suppose."

I said they didn't usually. He agreed with a good-humoured growl. " Recall 'em to quarters," he said and began to beat tattoo on the steering-wheel with his gloved hands. Ceasing this, he looked at me searchingly. " Family council, perhaps."

" Why ? "

" Don't know why. No special reason. Rose been a bit on edge of late, don't you think ? "

" I haven't seen much of her," I replied, truly enough.

" No. I suppose not. Still. . . . What do you think of her ? " he exclaimed suddenly. The question was asked not of me, but of himself. He didn't care a damn for the little boy's opinion, but asked it, nevertheless, as he might have done if I had happened to be beside him while he was contemplating a risky purchase at a shop. " D'you like her, I mean ? "

" Yes."

" A bit up and over," he said. " Still, a good girl, really. Good for keeps. The fizzy ones often are. . . . Great thing about Rose is, she don't want *you* to fizz. Look at that picnic-party. . . . Sound gal, really. Jog along. Give an' take. Never makes me uncomfortable for long. 'Shall I hold your high horse while you dismount?' I said to her once. You should have seen her. Laughed like a good 'un. Came off at once."

He was, in his blundering way, gathering confidence in his decision. What shocked me was his belief that he had only to decide. It seemed to me that I knew more about it than he did. His lazy arrogance — the more arrogant because he didn't see it so — shocked me. The blood came into my cheeks. I thought out nothing. Flinging all judgement to the winds, I was a boy again and passionately on Howard's side, so I kept my mouth shut and pretended to be interested in the horseless chariot.

Suddenly Matho sprang into life. The front door was open on the hot day; he must have seen Rapp passing through the hall, for he called and flourished an arm. Rapp came out to the steps.

"Oh, Rapp, tell Miss Rose I called and couldn't wait any longer."

"Very good, my lord."

"Tell her — oh, well, say I was sorry to miss her."

"I'll give the message, my lord."

Matho climbed down and applied himself to the starting-handle.

"Never does to wait for ever," he said. "Makes you look a fool."

When the car was gone, I looked round to ask Rapp my question, but Rapp by then was far away in his own pantry.

My question, which troubled me deeply because there appeared to be no possible answer to it that made sense, I hugged to myself. How had Dick Featherford suddenly become " my lord "? It was a question to ask my father privately, if I wanted not to make a fool of myself, for he never laughed at questions. My first chance to be safely alone with him was on our daily walk to school and railway station next morning.

" Well," he said, " he is a lord now. His father died and he succeeded to the title. He is Lord Comberagh."

" But why, if his name is Featherford ? "

" Oh, come, David," my father said smilingly, rather pleased, I think, to catch out ' the scholar of the family ', " where's your history ? What was the Duke of Marlborough before he was Marlborough ? "

" Churchill."

" And Wellington before he was Wellington ? "

" Wellesley."

" And Master Dick was Featherford before he was Comberagh. One's the family name, the other's the title."

" I see," I said, but doubtfully, because other questions were leaping up in my head. I was remembering confusedly an earlier conversation with my father.

" Well," he said, " what's the trouble ? "

" Comberagh . . . was that the name you said before ? You remember, Father, ages ago, when you told me about Mrs. Letterby ? "

" The peer who died was her brother."

" Then that makes him Miss Letterby's uncle ? "

" It does indeed."

Suddenly I saw a happy ending to the story. The ogre had been removed. Letterby Manor was saved. " Then that means that Morgy Gee, I mean the mortgagee, is dead — is really *dead* ? " I exclaimed with enthusiasm.

" Oh no, it doesn't," my father answered. " Mort-gagees never die. Comberagh was and Comberagh is."

I began to understand now to what this was leading. We had reached the station; it was time to part; there was little time for questions.

" Father," I said, fast and breathlessly, " on the day of the funeral Mr. Letterby said — we were having tea, Miss Letterby was there — and he said something about—" I paused, trying to remember.

My father, who had been turning away, was interested now. " What did he say ? "

" Something about a ' pack of lawyers '. He didn't blame them. He said they'd have to ' press now '. Press for what ? "

" Their money."

" And sell up the Manor ? "

" Maybe."

" But isn't that horrible and wicked and — and vile ! "

" Steady, steady," my father said; " it often happens, when someone dies and an estate passes, there are death-duties to pay — and debts, who knows ? They can't let things slide. They have to get their money in."

His explanations were without effect. The thing was horrible, wicked, vile. All day it grew in my mind, a storm of baseness and injustice, coming between me and my books. Now I knew why Matho had been so sure of himself and had patted the steering-wheel with huge, complacent hands. I hated him; I hated his gross motor-car, *plena ipso*, bulging with himself.

27

THE immediate sequel is not proud telling, but has to be told. My motive was admirable, my understanding incomplete, my action precipitate. Not boys only have made fools of themselves for these three reasons. Throughout life they go together. Let the account be brief.

At the next opportunity I knocked at the door of Rose's sitting-room and asked, a little formally, for an audience. She appeared not to notice the formality but was lightly glad to see me, and this lightness was itself disconcerting, for I had come to play a tragic or, at least, a romantic part, and had rehearsed my opening words a thousand times. . . . I have come to tell you, I was to say, something I think you ought to know.

She was, as I know now but did not then, in that condition of unhappiness in which unhappiness rebels against itself. Anything to escape from the boredom of being self-divided! Anything for release from the turgid contradictions of delight and common sense! If I had been a grown man, how perilous she would have been, and how vulnerable! If I had been a priest, how submissive! As I was a boy so evidently in love with her, how interested, how tentative, how wan — but with what swift colour — and how amused!

She gave me no chance for my opening line. In a

moment I was beside her on the window-seat. On a table was tea. She found another cup — a great mug from the mantelpiece — but it seemed to me my duty not to eat or drink. I have come to tell you . . . but it was impossible. She talked. I sat and gazed.

" Oh," she said, " I have been good. I have done what you told me. I can play that mazurka now, not just the opening bars, but right through. Shall I ? "

After it she played more Chopin, more and more. Waltzes.

" You see," I began, " if you—"

She came over and touched me. " What are you trying to say ? You are a funny one. Say it. I'm listening."

" If you," I began again with a sense that my life was sliding away from me down a glacier because I wasn't old enough to hold it, " if you . . . really wanted to be . . . no, I mean, if you believed it, you could be——"

" Don't say ' a great musician '. It's just not true."

" I wasn't going to say that ! I was going to say——"

" Oh," she answered quickly, " no one believes that but you," and then, not knowing, perhaps, whether she had been harsh or kind, she sat down at the piano again and played nonsense violently.

I was content to watch.

When the noise subsided, I said : " Please play the mazurka again."

" Why ? "

" Because——"

" Because you ask it ? . . . Very well. Very well. God knows, it's reason enough. As good a reason as I shall ever have for doing anything."

While she was playing, I saw her more clearly — I mean, in sharper physical outline and more precise definition of colour — than I had ever seen her before, but at a great distance and in complete isolation. None of her surroundings existed; she was no longer Miss Letterby, nor was I Ann's brother or my father's son; her single being rhymed with mine in a world without acts or hours.

"Where are you now?" I heard her say. "In Poland, dancing my mazurka?"

Though I had not taken my eyes off her face, I had, it seemed, not noticed that the mazurka was done or that she had been sitting — for how long? — with her hands on her lap, watching me. I blushed in fear of having been discourteous, remembering that, if a lady played the piano to you, it was necessary to thank her and pay her some compliment, if you could think of one. Nothing came. I could think of nothing at first except that I was in the same room with her. There was nothing I wanted to say or do. While she played I had forgotten that there was any reason for my being here and even that time was passing. Now I had a vision of myself going out of the Manor with nothing said and all my decisions to make again.

"Is it true," I asked, "that you are going away?"

"Why do you ask that?" she said, in so strained a voice that I knew she had misunderstood me and was thinking of Howard.

"I meant," I explained, "you and your father."

She sighed with relief. "Why should we?"

"He said, on the day of the funeral, something about——"

"So he did. I'd forgotten you were there."

" Then it is true ? "

" I don't know. Perhaps. I never believe that anything will happen until it does."

This casualness of hers, her continuing even now to shrug her shoulders at everything, confirmed me in my view that she was being deceived. How could she continue to have dealings with a man who, for the sake of " getting his money in ", was prepared to drive her and her father out of their home ? I looked round the room and saw it as it would be after the sale, dismantled like my card-room downstairs, emptier perhaps — the piano gone — neither she nor I would be sitting here — she and her father would be wandering about dark lanes in driving rain ; they would knock on doors, no one would answer ; I should never see her again.

" What is the matter ? " she said, " are you bothered about something ? Is it your French, or what ? "

" It's not me," I said, " it's nothing to do with me ! " I had a terror that she was going to comfort me, that she might even take me in her arms. If that happened, everything would fail. I should be reduced to the level of a boy, powerless to save her.

" I have come to tell you," I said, twisting myself away from her and looking out of the window, " something I think you ought to know."

Even she was arrested by the solemnity of that. " What is it ? " she asked.

The tree-tops were bowing in leafy tumult. Blown rooks were tumbling — what was Tennyson's phrase ? The first large drops of a shower splashed on the panes.

I nerved myself and said : " Do you know what Matho is ? "

" What do you mean — *what* he is ? He isn't anything."

" He is a Morgy Gee."

" What on earth is that ? "

Then I had been right. She didn't know. Howard himself didn't know. No one would ever have told her. I turned round, trembling for her wrongs.

" It's quite horrible. It's a kind of money-lender, but much worse." I began in a quiet, explanatory, grown-up way, but excitement gathered, my voice rose. " It's a money-lender who — who gets — who gets his claws into people's homes and drives them out, and sells everything — your piano, your father's books, everything — and then, of course, he makes them do whatever he wants, they are like serfs, and you—"

Her wondering look arrested me and shot me through with my first misgiving.

" Do you hate him so ? "

" How can I help it ? I——"

" But, David, he hasn't done anything."

" It isn't what he's done. It isn't even what he will do. It's what he *is*."

At that moment, he was indeed not Matho any more, the thick-skulled ninny who had taken me for a drive, but a monstrous and evil presence to be exorcized. I was not thinking of the man, but looking at her just as one looks at a cherry-tree in blossom and remembers with incredulity the angry howling of a mob ; I was pierced by the sense she awoke in me of there being behind the confusion of her life, of life itself — behind our contrary loves, ambitions, longings, our divisions by circumstances and age, behind our dryness, our swirling dust — something quite simple and cool. And as I looked at her, my anger went out of me. The excited, indignant tone I had used became an ugly noise; I wanted to cancel it, but it echoed on stupidly. She was looking back at me in amazement, aware, I suppose, that I had been struggling to do something for her sake but not in the least knowing what it was.

" David," she said, " listen : are you telling me that he — his father really — has a mortgage on the place ? I have always known that." And in answer to my speechlessness : " But of course I have ! It has been Father's obsession for years. . . . It isn't Matho's fault. Someone had to lend the money. . . . Sit down again peacefully and talk to me."

I sat down, listening to the rain. She sat beside me, and talked me gently away from my humiliation. It was I who returned to it.

" I thought it was wrong," I said.

" You mean — to lend money ? "

" Not that exactly. . . . It's you. It gives him power over you."

" But, David, he wouldn't use it that way. He isn't a beast."

" No."

" You mustn't hate him."

" I don't now." Whether she smiled then or not, and, if she smiled, what she was smiling at, I do not know, but something in her expression, or in her communicated thought, drove from me words that had been so little formed in my mind that they appalled me when I had spoken them : " You think I am jealous. I'm not. It's not true. Really, really, I'm not, because of course I know that I . . . am so young . . . that—"

She remained still, following a raindrop with her finger.

" Whatever happens," she said, " try not to despise me. There'll probably be plenty to despise." As she stood up, her skirt swept my knees. " Look," she continued, " this storm has made it dark. Will you help me light the lamp ? "

We went to the table together. I took off the shade and the chimney and waited for her to strike a match, but the box came over to me with a little dry rattle. I was so glad to be doing something that I became happy again. As soon as the lamp was lighted, I began to walk about the room with a kind of possessiveness. I alone loved her as she wished to be loved. Whatever happened, I should never despise her. When I was old — forty or forty-five perhaps — I should remember the smell of the oil-lamp which now was in my nostrils. When she came away from the cupboard — I looked over my shoulder at her stooping figure — I would tell her this, and I began to rehearse the words in which to tell her.

She came towards me with a rustling box.

" Look, David, have one of these."

They were chocolates.

" Put some in your pocket."

Only little boys put sweets into their pocket, but I could not refuse ; I thought it would humiliate her if I did.

28

Early in July the time came for me to face my examination at Eton. My sister accompanied me, enduring great inward stress and yet, perhaps, relieved, as I was, by our enforced isolation from the events at home. There were nine papers, each of two hours. The examination lasted three days. After work, each evening we walked down to the river and playing-fields, I telling her of my fortunes and misfortunes, she glad to have her mind drawn away into a subject so remote and impersonal.

Some of the candidates we met — Tony Seaford among them — regarded the whole affair as an outing; others were miserably anxious and exhausted. I lived, for the most part, in a condition of exaltation, as though stimulated by a drug. As I went into Upper School and took my place in the great room, and stared at the panels carved with so many names and at the pedestalled busts surmounting the panels, as I listened to the preliminary shuffling of feet, the rustle of papers, the click of penholders, I would select, from among the busts, my patron for the hours ensuing — Gray, Shelley, Porson for my Greek, and once, because he was above one of the pulpits and had a kindly face, Canning. As soon as the questions were in my hands, I passed through a period, lasting perhaps sixty seconds, in which I was afraid to read them; then, in a state of trembling self-control, plunged.

As long as I was writing, all else on earth cast out, I was happy, seldom troubled even by the pressure of time; but, when the paper was done and I returned to consciousness of an external world, it was a return to terror; precious hours had dropped out of my life and I had wasted them. The active terror died soon; even while it lasted I knew it to be nervous and exaggerated; much worse was my understanding, as paper followed paper, that I was losing ground.

In my General Paper, which embraced History and Divinity among the many questions from which we might select, I was led astray. Discreetly avoiding the examiners' curiosity about the working of an electric bell, of which indeed I knew nothing, I observed with relief that, lower on the same page, they wished to know what I understood by the Kingdom of Heaven. This escape from applied science beckoned me. I understood only too much by the Kingdom of Heaven. Not only did I rehearse the relevant parables, for which the examiners asked, and tell them about Jeremy Taylor whose *Golden Grove* was in the Squire's library, but I gave them the benefit of my own original thought on the subject, which was certainly more poetical than orthodox. When my zealous pen had disposed of the Kingdom of Heaven, I looked at my watch. Two-thirds of my time was gone. Everything else was scamped. Wolsey's ambition was put away in a paragraph; the Persian invasion of Greece in 480 B.C. ended with a wild scrawl in mid-sentence. Theology had been my undoing.

Latin Unseens were almost as disastrous. I did well, finished early and walked out, only to discover, when it was too late, that, because I had tackled the passages in my own order, I had omitted one to which I had intended to return. It was one of those aberrations of a mind in stress for which there is no accounting.

Latin verse was my only consolation, and even that was hazardous. That morning a treble-choir in a near-by practice-room, which had haunted us on other days with its clearly audible chants, was singing with rare sweetness. The music was in my head as I studied a poem set for translation into Latin elegiacs. It began :

> *In vain to me the smiling mornings shine,*
> *And reddening Phoebus lifts his golden fire . . .*

and at first it pleased me little. It seemed stiff, repetitive, and clumsy in its rhymes. The poet, whom I did not then know to be Gray, was saying that the delights of Nature — the sunrise, the bird-song, the cheerful green of the fields — were no longer delightful to him in the absence of the friend whose death he mourned ; and I, who had been hoping for a lyric of Keats, was disappointed by poetry in so conventional a dress. But, as I read the sonnet again, I was suddenly held and enchanted by the second of the four concluding lines :

> *The fields to all their wonted tribute bear ;*
> *To warm their little loves the birds complain :*
> *I fruitless mourn to him that cannot hear,*
> *And weep the more, because I weep in vain.*

The examiner had added a footnote, intended to be helpful, in which he said : " The word ' loves ' may be translated by *pares* (mates) ", and this footnote challenged me. It seemed shockingly dull and pedestrian. Surely, I said to myself, the tenderness of " to warm their little loves " deserves a less neutral word than *pares*! The choristers' singing came through closed doors as though it were being poured down from an open sky upon me alone. I had the strange sense, which has come since then in dreams, of being dictated to by a voice of which the precise accents could just not be caught by effort and attention; but the voice was an undertone to my own endeavour, and I performed two acts at the same time: I struggled intellectually, selecting words, shaping verses, and I listened, receiving something — a murmur, a colour, a boldness — from outside myself. The last four lines were written first :

> *dat solitas campus fruges ; parvisque volucris*
> *deliciis " grato sim tibi grata " canit.*
> *nil ego proficiens surdas suspiria in aures*
> *do, magis et, vanum est quod mihi flere, fleo.*

The rest followed.

I came out glowing.

" My elegiacs ! " I said to Ann. " I wish you could read them. I have a copy. I wish you could ! I wish you could ! "

But she was not a Latinist, and my joy in them faded. One paper could not save me among nine.

29

Dᴜʀɪɴɢ the week-end that followed our return from
Eton, I walked about the house and garden with my
examination papers, and such notes of my answers as
I had been able to make, bulging my pockets. I ached
to talk to someone about what had been the climax of
so long an endeavour. Nothing remained to do. For
once in my life, my books were out of action; all work
was now " too late ". I was haunted by remembrances
of chances missed, above all by my having wasted my
time on the Kingdom of Heaven and by my crass
stupidity in leaving out a chunk of the Latin Unseens,
and yet, if I could have talked about the exam — as
an actor, seeking the consolation of fragmentary
praises, will sometimes talk about a performance in
which he has failed — I should have kept the door of
the past ajar.

Howard was in no mood for my troubles. Ann,
certainly, had had enough of them. I would not go to
Mr. Letterby yet. Therefore I fell back on my father.
As he knew neither Latin, Greek, French nor ancient
history, there was not much except mathematics to
talk to him about, but he was an anchorage for my
agitated mind. Not that he took lightly my report of
failure. Having never failed himself in anything he
set his hand to, and entertaining no high opinion of the
" average intelligence ", he clearly regarded it as an

oddity of fate that a son of his should not excel; but he accepted the fact stoically, spoke no word of blame, said he had no doubt I had done my best and no one could do more, and added — contrary to the belief he had implanted in me — that, though I should fail to go to Eton as a scholar, I should go there nevertheless at his sole expense.

" Indeed," he said, " I have already made arrangements."

This was a consolation to me, but also a shock. Arrangements for a boy's going to Eton were not to be made at the last moment; my father must have secured my line of retreat long ago. For the first time I grasped how fully he had accepted my schoolmaster's low estimate of my powers; he must have written off my chances of a scholarship when I was quite a little boy, and all he had said to me about " a rung in the ladder " had been said without substantial hope. Did he really think I was a fool? Had he the least notion of how high the standard of an Eton scholarship was? To be quietly ranked by him as a mediocrity was more than I could bear.

He was sitting, as his habit was on Sunday afternoons in summer, in an upright wicker armchair under an acacia-tree. He had been reading, as his habit was on Sunday afternoons that summer, *Great Expectations*, which he already knew by heart, and which he read again and again in the ever-frustrated hope that next time it would end differently. I was on the grass beside him. Because he embodied for me whatever good may be in the wisdom of the world, I desired passionately to convince him that I was not the ineffectual incompetent he thought me. But the evidence I could produce — except the Maths answers which promised me eighty-five per cent — meant little to him, and my Latin verses, for which I was sure Virgil would have rewarded me with a friendly tweak of the ear, less than nothing. Nevertheless, on the principle that all I did had interest for him, he went through every paper in turn, giving me the impression now as always that, in success or failure, I had in him an unswerving ally.

When there was no more to be said on the subject of my scholarship, I asked him about his own journey. He was going to a Railway Conference in Paris and, by a sudden decision of which nothing had been said before our going to Eton, was taking Ann with him. Why was he taking Ann?

" Oh, I thought it would be a change for her," he said in that final and evasive tone which implied other reasons not for my ear.

" Is it for long ? "

" Only a few days."

During those few days Howard and I would be alone in the house. Little did I think then in what way, or how deeply, I should be alone, but the prospect of my father's and my sister's absence vaguely troubled me, for I had observed since my return a change in Howard.

The depression that had fallen on him after the river picnic was gone ; he was alert, spoke with his old vigour, moved with a quick step. The weather-vane moods which had succeeded his depression were gone likewise, and I said to myself: perhaps it's all over, perhaps he has gone back to his work again. But he was doing no more work than he was compelled to do. I watched him almost with alarm. His former energy, his decisiveness, which came near to being fanatical, had returned, but what had he decided? To marry Rose? That I knew to be impossible. Neither had money; he had his way to make; the notion of a long, patient engagement between him and her was fantastic even to my romantic mind. Besides, if that was the decision they had reached, would it not at least have given him peace? Years of waiting might stretch ahead, but to wait seemed to me then a proof and justification of marriage. And there was no peace in Howard. A fixity of purpose, a self-disciplined calm, but not peace.

It is impossible to convey the impression he made on me at that time otherwise than by confessing to an absurdity. I awoke in the middle of that Sunday night. My first thought was the wild one that my Latin elegiacs had saved me; the examiners would have said: whatever his faults may be, we can't reject a boy whom Virgil would have tweaked by the ear. My second thought was that Howard had made up his mind to commit suicide — " on Tuesday ", I said to myself. If he had decided to commit suicide on Tuesday, would not everything be explained? I jumped out of bed, half asleep. But one cannot go into a man's room on Sunday night to find out whether he will commit suicide on Tuesday.

I jumped back and began to laugh under the bed-clothes, and yet — for all inconsistences are possible — I was frightened. Ann and my father would be in Paris on Tuesday night. Tuesday, Tuesday, Tuesday, I said, and put out my head to stare at the pale-blue window, for in summer my curtains were drawn back. What would happen, I thought, if another porter came and threw gravel at the window? Father wouldn't be able to go to Paris. Ann would stay, and all be well. But no porter came, though I ardently expected him, and I fell asleep.

Next day took me to school, for, though there was no more for me to learn there, my fees had been paid and my daily attendance was to continue until the term ended. The travellers' luggage was in the hall. I said good-bye to them before I set out, surprised and pleased to find that Ann was light-hearted in the prospect of her journey.

"What are you going to do with yourself, David, while we are away? Now your scholarship is over, you're rather in the air, aren't you?"

"Oh," I said, "don't you worry about me. . . . And, Ann, if there's a play by Molière, go to it if you get a chance, and tell me about it because . . ."

I was talking to put off, moment by moment, my parting from her. As I did so, I became certain that a phase in our lives had ended and that, when we met again, everything would be changed. This certainty was intuitive, not reasoned; I had no premonition of what was to happen, but I dragged her into the garden as far as the gate and found it hard even then to let go of her.

School was barren. The four of us who had sat for a scholarship were summoned by Mr. Libbett to a jocular *post-mortem*. Tony Seaford and I were left to the last. The other two, meek boarders, gave earnest accounts of themselves, pleasing Mr. Libbett by their evidence that they had made good use of his " quirks ".

"And you, Seaford," he said, " devoted your mind to cricket, I suppose?"

Tony said with a cheerful grin that his Latin-into-

English hadn't been so bad and his Maths was
" decent ", but as for the rest . . .

" Did you copy any of your answers ? "

" No, sir."

" Then you were pretty busy, writing up to the last
moment ? "

" No, sir."

" But if you had time to spare, why didn't you copy
your answers ? "

Tony was silent but unembarrassed. " Well, sir,"
he said, " there were the most frightful gaps and if——"

" I see," Mr. Libbett broke in ; " well, we shan't
break our hearts, shall we ? " And, leaving the rest of
us to our own devices, he talked to Tony about the
Etonian mysteries which would be his without a
scholarship, and slapped him on the back and used all
the jargon he could lay his tongue to. " And now,"
he said, turning to me at last, " what did the Professor
make of it all ? "

A stubborn and bitter wrath possessed me. Why
should I confess my failures in scholarship to a man
whose job was to teach and who yet despised scholarship in his heart ? I would tell him nothing.

" Oh, I don't know, sir," I said, falling back on a
boy's privilege to be inarticulate ; and this, which was
unexpected in me, who had so often infuriated him by
earnestly bubbling over about my work, set his eyes
alight. He interpreted my silence as abject failure and
I saw that he was glad.

" Come," he said, " what was the good of excusing
you cricket all this term if you have no more to tell me
than that ? "

I mentioned some of the papers and made evasive

comments on them, which strengthened his impression that I was trying to conceal a complete rout. The others were staring at me. Mr. Libbett assumed a tone of grave and almost purring sympathy.

" Come," he said again, " no one wants to hit a man when he's down. Some of the best scholars have had a kind of — a kind of nervous seizure at the crucial moment. A friend of mine — years ago now — better scholar than myself — handed in blank papers."

" Oh, I didn't do that, sir."

" What was it then ? "

" Nothing."

He patted my shoulder. " May not be as bad as you think. Did you keep no copies ? "

A proud contrary devil then possessed me.

" One, sir," I said, and handed him my elegiacs. I knew the quality of those verses and that it wasn't by the rules a schoolboy quality. They were correct, but they were also odd, as if, while I wrote them, someone with a style had been whispering in my ear. I knew them by heart now. The more often I had mumbled them to myself and the farther I had drawn away in time from the desk at which they had been written, the less did they seem to belong to me. They were my humility rather than my pride ; they took my breath away ; what their effect on examiners would be I didn't know — except that they were hit or miss ; and no sooner had I put them into Mr. Libbett's hands than I disliked myself for having done so. Nevertheless, I watched his face. It was uncomfortably puzzled.

" Well, yes," he said, " very pretty, very pretty. . . . But if I've told you once I've told you a hundred times : examiners expect you to hold tight to the original. Let a word slip and they think you don't know the word. Stick to copy and make your verses scan. Poetry and so on can go to blazes. They are not asking you to be a poet." He picked up a red pencil and began to underline: " *This*, for example, and *this* — a pretty turn I grant you — but it isn't what they are asking for *from you*. . . . Still," he added, almost reluctantly, " it's correct as far as it goes. They'll give you credit for that."

30

To get the taste of school out of my mouth, I turned in at the Manor on my way home. The sun beat directly on my shoulders as I passed through the lion-gates, and the avenue stretching ahead was almost shadowless. It was a blazing day, so hot that even after a laggard climb of Farthing Hill my feet were swollen in my boots and my eyes had begun to ache and itch.

By plunging through the bushes on my left I came into a twisting path beside which, in small semi-circular bays, there stood at intervals curved stone seats, each on a platform of two shallow steps. They were cracked now, patched with moss and overgrown with ivy. No one came this way; even I was a rare visitor; but I liked the path with its soft tread, its brambly entanglements, its close-stooping trees that made a tunnel of it here and there, and its appearance, which those carved seats gave it, of having once been elegant and clipped.

Smaller paths led out of it, to form, at the heart of the wood, a little system which, on an old estate-plan in the Squire's room, was called Lady Sara's Maze. Except that Lady Sara had been his great-grandmother, and that the " Chinese pagoda " shown on the plan in a central clearing had never existed, he could tell me nothing of it. " I suppose she grew tired of it or died," he had said. " Money wasted. Nothing done." But I at least was grateful to Lady Sara. Her jungle was cool, and I found it pleasant to establish myself on one of her stone seats and, for the first time since my examination, be glad of idleness.

When the damp sound of my palm detaching itself from the stone was sound no longer, none other followed but a finger-nail's click on a button. There fell by chance one of those intervals of silence, rare in the country, most rare in woods, which for a hovering instant awe the mind by their absolute void. Even the small wood-whisperings were hushed ; no leaf turned nor twig snapped ; there was not the lift of a feather or the hop of a wren. A blur of midges swung up and down, into and out of a hard beam of sun, so deepening the silence by the silence of their fretful activity that there became nothing to listen for except the turning of the earth ; but I heard only, deep in my breast-pocket, where it hung by a leather strap, my own watch, never before audible at that unfathomable depth, which had begun to tick, with an infinitely remote distinctness, like a huge clock on the other side of the world.

Then arose, among the reviving murmur of the wood, a far vibration of voices, now eager, now hushed, now pitched on a note of anguish, now faded into a long, inexplicable pause. Not yet words, only the flutter, the delight, the stress of haste, the little cries of a wild secrecy, the crackle of feet.

Then words — Howard taut in argument :

" But if he went to your father at all, he must at least have had the idea that—" The rest of the sentence and her answer were lost. I started up, caring only not to interrupt and embarrass them, but was still on the lower of the two steps when his voice, confident and exalted but thickened as though there were dust in his throat, rose on the singly audible word :

" To-morrow ? "

" Oh yes, yes, I have promised, I have said . . ."

" You won't fail ? "

Some answer perhaps. After it silence. I fled along my path, seeing as I went, deep in the shadow of the Maze, the backward curve of a white dress, like a scimitar among the trees.

The path I was following debouched, after many turnings and twistings, in the carriage-sweep before the house, where, drawn back into the shade of the central oak, the carriage itself somnolently gleamed. The reins were slack ; one of the horses was idly snuffing among the oak-roots and finding nothing ; when I looked up I saw that the coachman was nodding, a curly-brimmed hat having slid forward over his eyes. My curiosity became at once irresistible. The carriage was so old and so strangely shaped that it ranked in my imagination with the carriages and sedan-chairs I had seen once in a museum. There they had rested, for ever immobilized and empty on their numbered stands. Who had last travelled in them? On what errand? What had been said, what done? Above all, what had it felt like to be swung in them and to look out from those windows at the normal coming and going of passers-by? A small boy then, I had begged to be allowed to climb in and been forbidden. Now, urged by the same impulse, I approached the Letterby carriage cautiously from the rear, coming up on its off-side, between it and the house.

Its enamel, seen close, was lined by delicate fissures of a hair's breadth, with the effect of crackle in a black porcelain; the silver door-handle, moulded to the Letterby crest, was smoothed by the clutch of innumerable fingers. Would it creak? It turned so loosely that the danger was a rattle of the socket, but this was avoided by slow and discreet pressure. . . . Would the hinge complain? The door came back as though it were slung on air. . . . Not daring, lest the carriage should rock, to mount by the step, I crawled in with elaborate precaution, only to reflect, with the smell of the floor-rug in my nostrils, that I must certainly be the first to enter on hands and knees, and to be plunged into stifling peril of laughter. Nevertheless, I righted myself, closed the door and slid back into a place of honour facing the horses.

The cushions were harder and the seats, with their curving sides, lower and wider than I had expected. I had an impression of being in the cabin of a funereal boat, musty with black draperies and studded with small fittings of ivory. But apart from a slipping of fingers into mysterious slots and pockets, which might with luck be holsters, and brief examination of an inlaid corner-bracket above my head and a shallow cupboard under the seat opposite, I wasted no time in twentieth-century curiosity, but lay back with arms folded to enjoy a journey through the plains of Lombardy which would bring me by easy stages to Rome.

One afternoon, a little before dusk, we were approaching the gates of Florence — if indeed Florence had gates — when Mr. Letterby said: " Well, my dear Farrow, I'm glad we've had this little preliminary talk. It was good of you to come at short notice. It's always well to know one's ground."

A short, dome-headed man with varnished boots placed neatly together and a silk hat pressed to his hip, was standing, like a Noah's Ark figure, at Mr. Letterby's side under the portico.

" Then I'll go ahead quietly with a draft settlement," he said, " but I'll make no move until the other side does. Then there should be no difficulty. The other matter carries the mortgage on its back, provided——"

" I think it's firm enough," said Mr. Letterby doubtfully. " The boy came to me, solemn as an owl."

" Comberagh ? Oh, no doubt. Some puppies are by nature owls. But there are two sides to everything, particularly marriage. The question is: the young lady ? "

" Ah well, I've told you what I know myself. She asked why the boy came to *me* at that point. When I said it was customary, she only smiled and shrugged her shoulders, and——"

" Reserved her defence ? " Mr. Farrow suggested.

" Didn't say No, anyhow. Seemed amenable. I wish you'd seen her yourself."

" Oh no, oh no, oh dear no. A lawyer at this stage — a thousand times no. Don't show fillies the bridle. Besides, you don't want to use undue influence."

" True," said the Squire briefly, " but it's comfortable harness."

They began to move down the steps. The humiliation of being discovered in my childish game appeared to me hotly. There was still time to slip out of the carriage on the farther side, encircle the oak, and disappear, as the coachman awoke, down Lady Sara's Walk.

On my way, I met Rose. Her hair was disordered, her small teeth were brilliantly visible between parted lips, her cheeks flushed as though she had been dancing. She had a wild, exultant air, and yet, at sight of me, her eyes filled with uncontrollable tears. She brushed them aside with the back of her hand, petulantly, like a little girl.

" You! " she said. " You can't have been doing Greek to-day! I thought it was all over anyhow. . . . Have you seen my father ? "

" No."

" What have you been doing then ? "

" I turned back."

" It's funny, isn't it ? " she said. " It seems not to matter in the end. . . . Wouldn't it be a relief if everything just stopped, like a watch when you don't wind it ? Wouldn't it ? . . . Is that the carriage ? "

" I think so."

" Listen," she said, " I always like the moment when you can't hear wheels any more."

As we listened she took my hand.

Afterwards, letting me go, she asked : " Did you get your scholarship ? "

" No."

" No ? . . . Or do you mean you don't know yet ? "

" I don't officially know yet."

" When shall you ? This week ? "

" Soon. Not this week."

" What a long time. . . . Oh David, I do hope you get it ! I do hope and hope you get it ! "

This was spoken with such vehemence that I stared at that lovely, trembling face, and asked : " Why ? "

" Because," she said, " I should love you to be

peacefully happy. Someone ought to be. Why not
you? . . . Do you want to come in to tea?"

I shook my head and shook my head, unable to
speak. So we parted. I rounded a turn in the path,
then stood still, hoping to hear her footstep. It was
already gone.

That evening I sat through dinner with Howard.
Afterwards I saw him reckoning up the figures on the
counterfoils of his cheque-book. From under the lid
of the music-stool, I took the volume of duets which
he had given to Ann on her birthday, and left it about
before going to bed. It was not Ann only whom I was
trying to save, but Rose and Howard and myself. I
lay awake, staring at my knees drawn up and covered
by a sheet, and praying for deliverance from the
unreason into which our lives were being sucked down.
I knew little of what had happened and understood
little of what I knew. I desired lucidity, order,
simplicity: perhaps the volume of duets had stood for
these things in my mind. Words were no longer of
any use. When Howard came upstairs and stood a
long time beside my bed, I pretended to be asleep.

31

O n the following day, Tuesday, I started back from school when work was over without any wish to reach home. It was useless to go to the Manor. My scholarship was a failure which had gone stale; even the vanity that had made me hope for Mr. Letterby's praise of my Latin verses pricked me no more. My father and Ann were away; our house would be empty; the servants would stare at me. When Howard came home I should not know what he was thinking, and there would be no communication between us. All places were empty, all eyes sightless, all books unreadable; there was nothing to do and nothing to look forward to. I was in that pit of desolation into which the very young can fall, because their lives are deep and endless.

At the core of this loneliness was my feeling that Rose, who was the source of all the beauty I should ever know in the world, who held for me the divine within the profane, was lost. Not that she would marry or not marry; this I did not know, this I did not understand; in this she was beyond my reach, plunged in confusion. Not that. When I said without reason: I shall never see her again, I did not mean that I should not again see her face or her body or hear her voice, but that I myself had died.

Because I did not wish to reach home, I turned into

the railway station. A porter, who knew nothing of these things, was a friend of mine and at that hour a train was expected; I would watch it come and go. In the little hall of the station beside the empty fireplace, she was standing, a crocodile dressing-case at her feet. Her back was towards me, her head lifted as though she were staring at a framed time-table on the wall. The gloved fingers of her right hand, fastened on some edge or lapel of her clothing, tightened, gathering up the stuff into a knot, then released it, then gathered it anew. She looked up at the wall-clock and, a moment later, looked again, as though, in the torment of indecisive waiting, her eyes had failed to read the clock-face or her memory to hold what her eyes had read.

No one else was there. She had not heard the noise of my boots on the bare planks, but the cessation of their noise summoned her. Aware of being watched, she swung round. At sight of me, her eyes filled with the wonder of seeing a ghost, and she drew herself up — taller and taller, shrinking from me and yet advancing, like a wave that seems to withdraw before it breaks — and suddenly the wave of her curled and broke upon me, and she seized my hands and said:

" David, do something for me ? Will you ? Please, please ! "

" Yes," I said, " of course, anything."

" Take this ticket. . . . It's only a single. . . . Look, look, here's money for a return. I've no change. Look. Half a sovereign."

The train was coming in. The porter called : " London Bridge. Waterloo. Charing Cross ! "

" Oh, David, go ! "

" What am I to do? "

" At Charing Cross, in the circulating space, sticking out from the wall, there's a huge clock."

" I know."

" Howard will be there. Go to him and tell him — David, listen: say: ' Rose can't come '." Then she added very fast to herself: " No, that isn't honest. He would misunderstand that. Say: ' Rose isn't coming '."

" Never? " I asked.

She could not bring herself to say that word, but shook her head.

The train was in now. The platform, at a lower level than ourselves, was not in sight, but the rattling of the train had ceased. A door banged behind an alighting passenger.

" But, Rose——"

" Go, go," she said, urging me by my arm.

" But he's expecting you! You *were* going! " I looked at the crocodile dressing-case and the ticket in my hand.

" Only to tell him that I — oh, my dear, my dear, go quickly! "

I ran down the steps on to the platform and sprang in as the train moved. God knows what she went through when I was gone, or by what stages and in what desolation she toiled up Farthing Hill in that blazing heat, with the dressing-case handle cutting her fingers!

The ticket in my hand entitled me to travel first class. I was in a third class compartment. It seemed to me necessary to get out at the junction, move along the train, and promote myself for the rest of the journey.

Howard was under the clock, tight-lipped and watchful. He also had a bag at his feet. My school-cap must have marked me in the throng, for his face awoke to recognition of me almost as soon as I had seen him. He turned his back instantly, thinking, I suppose, that I must be accompanied by someone and that the encounter was, at that moment, to be avoided at all costs. But I took his sleeve, gave my message, and repeated it in his contorted face.

One falls, in the crises of life, into an untidiness of small actions which seem afterwards to be lying about on the floor of memory like things dropped there accidentally, one does not know why or by whom. No doubt Howard questioned me and I gave him the best account I could of what had happened, but I see clearly at first only a label on which was written : " Howard Treladdin, Paris *via* Calais ". I remember then a difficulty about a railway ticket, my wish to explain that I had already been given money for a ticket, a wild search in pockets where the half-sovereign was nowhere to be found, and my watching the sleeve of Howard's coat while he bought a ticket for me. I was to go home. We walked together on to a platform where a train was standing. Until I was in my seat I did not look at his face. There was a taut furrow in each of his cheeks, and at the sides of the furrow a rising up of the muscles in cramped, knotty ridges ; and, though his mouth was firm and his eyes were unblinking and hard, the skin of his forehead twitched with wide movements of furling and unfurling, as though, beneath the skin, there were some fierce irritation.

" You go home, David," he said. " Don't you

worry. Everything's all right." After an interval, he repeated this. "Don't you worry. Everything's all right," and said it several times without knowing that he had repeated himself. Intending passengers, hurrying by with early editions of the pink *Globe* and the green *Westminster* tucked under their arms, looked at the empty seats in the compartment where I sat alone, but something in Howard's face or mine sent them by.

The porters were closing the doors; ours was closed between us. Howard, left there, appeared as desolate as though he too were a boy, turning his head from side to side, looking at this and that, seeing nothing. The late-comers began to run. In one of the turnings of his head, his eyes encountered mine. I don't know what he saw there — a link perhaps with Rose, a likeness to Ann; perhaps only that I was not anonymous or blank as the rest of his world had become. He wrenched at the door-handle and, as the train drew out, flung himself on to the seat opposite mine. I shut the door, leaned out of the window and remained leaning out. Two or three minutes later, I was bound to speak. " We are coming into Waterloo. Someone may get in." He stood up and mastered himself; he even straightened his tie in the narrow mirror under the luggage-rack.

"All right," he said, "but keep them out if you can."

I hung in the window. No one came in. The train went on and still we were silent. No one came in at London Bridge. After that we were secure.

" What are you going to do, Howard ? "

" Fetch her," he said at once, but, as he spoke, I knew and he knew that it was untrue. His expression changed. He was not lying or bragging; his words expressed the intention of his mind, but, suddenly, not the drive of his imagination. For an instant there appeared in his eyes an unmistakable gleam of relief, of being returned to himself. It shocked me then; I was better prepared for romantic humiliation and despair; but I have since observed, in the face of a man who had tried and failed to kill himself, a corresponding willingness to rediscover the hated world. "If we had the capacity to go mad," Rose had said, "shouldn't we have gone mad by now?" They had driven themselves beyond their capacities, had whipped themselves into an ecstasy outside their natural interest, and had broken. So be it. The shock of reverse, the will to act and recover, were still agonizing and violent in Howard. He plied me with questions, clung to desperate hopes. If there was a ticket in her hand, she had meant to travel. If her intention had been only to meet him under the clock and tell him she had changed her mind, why had she brought a dressing-case? "Because," Howard answered as if he were reviewing evidence in a court of law, "she was prepared to be over-persuaded. Women are mad!" he exclaimed, "it isn't that they can't make up their minds; they carry half a dozen minds about with them, like half a dozen dresses; it's wild chance which they put on. . . . If I had seen her. . . . If I see her now, there's no reason on earth—"

But he didn't believe it, the future had altered. The heat of battle and the desire of it were still raging within him, but the campaign was over. He leaned back in his place and stared out of the window at the glistening rails, the leaping embankments. With a hand that felt its way along the bag at his side, he tore off the label and held it screwed-up in his palm.

When we reached home, he said: " I shan't go to the Manor to-night. Better to-morrow." But later that evening, he told me that he must go very early to chambers. " There's a great deal to put straight. There's still time, if I act at once."

" What shall I say," I asked, " if I see Rose ? "

" To-morrow ? Why should you see her ? "

" I may. I haven't shown Mr. Letterby my scholarship papers yet. I ought to. If I don't before long, he'll remember and send for me."

" Not to-morrow. . . . Poor David," Howard added, " this is hell for you. . . . If you *do* see her, say — well, tell her you met me, we came home, tell her nothing is decided, I must have time to think." He began to walk up and down the room quietly as he had in the old days. " You see, David," he said, " I can't throw away my practice for nothing. In one way or another, life has to go on."

32

The calm did not hold. On Thursday evening, after his return from London, the disappearance of Rose from his life became unbearable to him. He could keep silence no longer. Because there was no other listener, he talked to me, always about her, neither blaming her nor protesting his love of her nor in any way criticizing their relationship, but describing her for the sake of having her name still upon his lips, recalling what she had said and done on a hundred occasions of no special significance now, and compelling me to do likewise, as though by talking and talking of her we were keeping her alive. Then he tired suddenly and pulled his hand across his eyes. " Half the time, I don't know what I'm saying." But he had extraordinary self-discipline. He was like a man rescuing himself from a drug. " The horrible thing is," he said, halting on the edge of the lawn, " if I went now, across the dingle, I could be with her in five minutes. But I know what would happen. Everything would begin all over again. It was like a puzzle that keeps on falling off the table." And he turned away into the house. " I have been refusing briefs," he said. " In my position, that's drunken madness. And I have scamped opinions. Now — well, my God, at least there's work. Come up, David, and work at your table. I'll work at mine. We'll keep the door open. That will keep me at it."

" I haven't any work," I answered. Had he forgotten that my failure, too, was in the past ?

" Nonsense," he said, " an Eton scholarship, even
if you have failed, isn't the only fish in the sea. You
have the whole of Greek and Latin literature. Read
that."

He laughed for the first time in three days ; I too.

On Friday night the end came. I had brought with
me to the dinner-table a French picture-postcard on
which my father and Ann confirmed that they would
be home on Monday evening. We carried this with
us on our coffee tray into the garden.

" I shan't be here," Howard said. Not knowing
what to make of this, I was silent. " I sent a letter to
Rose from London to-day," he continued. " After I
had posted it — things always happen that way, and
in this case it's good ; it's a mutual release — anyhow, a
mutual acceptance of facts — our letters' crossing, I
mean. . . ." He broke off, having lost his thread ;
then, with arid determination, resumed : " After I had
posted my letter, a letter from her came into chambers
in which she said that she intended to marry Comberagh and that the announcement will be in *The
Times* on Monday. . . . A lot more, but no matter.
I'm not blaming her. She's retreating into her
possibilities as I am into mine. . . . Anyhow, David,
that is ended, and obviously, even from her point of
view, it's best that I shouldn't stay here."

" Why ? " I exclaimed. " If she's married, if she's
gone——"

" Listen, David. Let me talk a bit. You may be
right or wrong about that, but it isn't the point. I'm
going for a different reason. I——"

" What do you mean — ' going ' ? "

" I mean," he said, looking away from me, and compelling himself to speak, " leaving this house, not living here any more, not coming here again. . . . Look : in a way, you know more about this than anyone else on earth. You love us all. I mean Ann, Rose too. And you like me — anyhow, you can talk to Ann. Or you will be able to, later on. Don't say——"

" Don't say what ? "

" Don't say I love her. It's unsayable now, though it has always been true. That's why I must go. And, what is more, it isn't, *now*, even true. I'm dead inside. I don't love Ann or Rose or you or anyone. I'm useless except as a working machine, and even the machine wants oiling. But I want to behave like a sane human being, and to hang about here, your father's guest, clinging on — it just won't work, David. I've written a long letter to your father. When they come back. . . ." He saw that I was trying to interrupt. " Well ? " he said.

I thought then that he was wrong because I knew in what spirit Ann would receive him. I was clinging to the past, believing that if I could now speak the talismanic word which would persuade him to stay, the life I had known and loved would be remade ; but the past cannot be remade, there is no healing except by rest, no future except in the slow re-creative processes of time. I know now that he was not wrong. Perhaps, within me, I knew it then. Certainly I had no talismanic word. All I said was :

" But, Howard, how will you live ? "

" In rooms, in London."

" But you're poor."

222

" I shall live poor." Then he smiled with his old arrogant flicker. " But mark my words, I shan't be poor for long." The arrogance had less confidence than in the past. " I wonder," he said, " we all over-value the false in ourselves and under-value the true. And then, when we want to go home——"

" But, Howard, this is your home."

He looked at it. " It was," he said.

33

THAT night and next morning he packed and in the afternoon went away, leaving on the hall-table two letters, for my father and for Ann. I sat up, doing nothing, until one in the morning. On Sunday, because at all costs I must stop thinking the same thoughts, I took ten shillings in silver out of my money-box, put my examination papers into my pocket and went to the Manor. No one was there but Rapp.

"But where are they?" It was incredible that there should be so bright a sun in so empty a world.

"They have gone over to spend the week-end with his Lordship," Rapp said.

On a tray, among the waiting letters, was one addressed to Rose in Howard's writing. I took from my pocket four florins, a shilling and two sixpences which would enable me to keep her half-sovereign for ever.

"Mr. Rapp," I said, "would you give these to Miss Rose, please? I owe them to her."

The slowing of time, which is the consequence of unhappiness and solitude, reached in me then an extreme that I have never since known. All my memories dragged at me. I stood by the blackthorn, now a compact green mass wilted by July's heat, until the aching of my legs drove me on. At home I would not eat, and began to think insanely, saying to myself that when I was fifty and Rose fifty-five there would be little difference in our ages, and pursuing this dire arithmetic up and down the scale. On Monday morning I ate ravenously and went to school in a dream, repeating to myself, as something altogether ridiculous and meaningless, Howard's saying that life must go on — in one way or another, life must go on; for I saw nothing ahead. I seemed to have no identity, for my identity had ceased to be related to anything.

In the middle of afternoon school, the gross man with a pasty face and waxed moustache whom we called the Sergeant, came in and spoke to the master at the blackboard. The master shook the chalk out of the sleeves of his gown, spoke my name, repeated it sharply when I failed to answer, and told me to go to the headmaster in his study. The class tittered, for the summons could be the prelude to a caning. I sprang up startled, left the room, and, completely without curiosity, climbed the oilclothed stairs.

" Well," said Mr. Libbett, " you go on the board."

The words meant nothing to me at first. In the main schoolroom there were boards, called Honours Boards, on which were painted, for the benefit of inspecting parents, the names of those who had won scholarships. Slowly the possible meaning of the words dawned upon me, but I was afraid of being tricked, and made no answer.

" Don't be stupid. The Honours Board. You have your scholarship."

Mr. Libbett held out his hand and blew congratulations through his moustache. When I returned to the classroom there were nudges and questioning eyebrows, but I shook my head. Even when school was over, I said nothing, but made off as fast as I could, my heart bursting, my mind shot through with fantastic lightnings. I felt that a miracle had happened. Sometimes I halted in the dusty road to contemplate it, and looked at my own right hand to identify it as mine. The probability that I had in the normal way done well and earned my place did not then occur to me. I had been saved, I was convinced, by my Latin verses, which had been written by my hand but dictated by a power within me, not my own. All the way up Farthing Hill I was shouting hymns, but as I had no voice worthy of the occasion the shouting remained inside my head, a deep magic of gratitude for this salvation.

There was no one at home but the servants to hear my news, but I told the parlour-maid, because she was, after all, part of my home. To my astonishment she crowed and rocked in exclamatory delight, and scuttered away into the kitchen, crying " Master David's got his prize ! Master David's got his prize ! " and cook and the housemaid appeared in the passage, clapping their hands. I was half-way upstairs, but was drawn back into the kitchen, and given tit-bits as though I had been a little boy. " You won't send your food away to-night," cook said.

So they had noticed. It was my first ovation. I was inexpressibly happy.

Upstairs, seated on the edge of my bed, I took stock. Howard's letters to my father and Ann which, I supposed, were still lying in the hall, belonged to the past. I loved my father and sister no less, nor was I less aware of what Ann must suffer ; but we are self-preserving beasts, and I clung to the glory — no, to the solidity, the reality, the uncancellable achievement, which had appeared in my own life. Nothing could take away what had now been given me. If I went blind to-morrow, the achievement would stand. The wave which had so nearly carried us all away was passing me by; I had the ground again under my feet. To-night, when the travellers returned and Howard's going was discussed, this one thing would stand like a rock. My father's face would light; I should have the satisfaction of watching his surprise. "Well, bless my soul, well done! That's the first rung in the ladder."

To-morrow? I saw myself going to the Manor. It would be Tuesday. Mr. Letterby would have returned. He would look at my Latin verses. If he praised them — and he might not — I would say . . . and suddenly I remembered Rose.

"Remembered", as though she too belonged to the past! My own life had begun to beat again, like a reviving pulse. I looked at my table and my neglected books. If I was a scholar, there was work to be done.

As I moved across the room to my table, I caught sight of myself in the looking-glass. My school-cap, Libbett's, was still on my head. I removed it and, with a revolutionary gesture, threw it out of the window; but, being what I am, went down into the garden, flapped the dust out of it and folded it into my pocket before going into the road to watch for my father's and Ann's return.

My future was opening before me. It seemed odd that it should exist so brilliantly in me alone while my father and Ann and Howard and Rose were unaware of it.

I stood in the road listening for the sound of carriage-wheels.

34

My tale of these events was finished three nights ago. As it has been written in Ann's house, I gave it her to read, believing it complete and wishing, in any case, to give no more time to it, for I have work still to do on a set of lectures and the new term at Oxford is drawing near.

Nevertheless, there are a few pages I must add. It may be only weakness or hesitancy that tempts me to fiddle with a water-colour sketch which, with all its faults and follies, would be best left alone, but I feel that, though not willingly or in my heart, I may have been guilty of injustice towards Rose of a special kind. The shield of a goddess is not a gentle burden to impose on any woman's arm. My injustice, if I have been unjust, arises not from over-emphasis on her faults — they were, I am afraid, in large measure the converse of my own — but, on the contrary, from my having, in the mood of over forty years ago, romanticized her too much and so laid her open to a charge of having failed to live up to claims which, in fact, she never made for herself. That injustice I wish to correct. It will be hard, for it is always hard to tell the truth in terms of this world without seeming to repudiate a vision no less true. Hence the quarrel between realists and romantics which, if they would but see it, is not a quarrel at all. Neither mask nor face is a lie.

My sister is the only person I have known whose mask and face have seemed to me identical. She is what she appears to be; she is undivided, and so peaceful to be with that I find her presence in a room a help even when I am writing. At this moment, she is within five yards of me, in her chair beside a summer fire.

When she gave me back my manuscript this morning, I had hoped that some word of hers might have given me a lead into what I have now to say. But it did not happen so. She gave me the papers with a smile and, I think, reservation of comment. It has never been her habit to make swift judgements. All she did at the moment was to advise me not to show my manuscript to Howard. "You see," she said in explanation, "he has never been Lord Chancellor or Lord Chief Justice or made a great fortune — partly because he genuinely outgrew the want of those things. He and I have been the happier in our marriage for that reason, or so I think, but his reasons may not be quite the same as mine. He may still remember sometimes that a County Court Judge isn't at the top of the tree." She put her hand on my manuscript as if it were a book she had closed. "There's nothing to be gained," she said, "by reminding people of their might-have-beens."

I am not sure that she was referring only to the Lord Chancellorship.

Since the last words were written the evening has passed, and I return to my page with the feeling that perhaps, after all, I am not the best person in the world to add a critical vindication of Rose Letterby. As I wrote " Lord Chancellorship ", Ann looked up from her embroidery and asked what I was writing now — an epilogue or a letter ?

Her face had that amused, quizzical expression which it has so often worn when she has suspected me of too solemnly wasting time. I defended myself.

" They may be much the same thing," I answered. " A letter to my own youth perhaps, and in a sense a letter to Rose as well."

" To Rose ?. And is she to read it ? Am I ? "

That question astonished and shook me. " But, Ann, you know she is dead ! "

The embroidery went down on to my sister's lap. " Dead," she answered slowly. " When ? Where did she die ? "

" At Cannes. The news was published just before I began to write all this. It was what made me write it."

" Did Howard see it ? He didn't mention it to me."

" Nor to me, Ann. But he reads his newspaper."

" I ought to," she said for the thousandth time. " What a queer family we are with our reticences — the things we don't say to one another. . . . Poor Rose ! . . . And yet, I don't know why I say that. I gather that, as such things go, the marriage wasn't unsuccessful. Even if I had been completely detached—" My sister broke off her sentence and looked out into the room before continuing : " I still think of *him*," she said, " by your name : Matho, with that explosive motor-car of his ! He was cheerful and easy-going and certainly he adored her. . . . What will he do now, I wonder. Stay at Cannes? It's often that kind of dullish man who is most utterly lost and lonely."

I was not interested in Matho, but in the sentence Ann had left unfinished.

" I was going to say," she began, in reply to my question, " — but it was a silly thing to say, perhaps an unkind one, I hardly know—"

I wanted her interpretation of the story, and pressed her for it.

" Only," she went on in her considering voice, " that if I had been completely detached and advising her for her own happiness, I think I should have given her, about the husband for *her* to choose, the advice which — well, which in the end she gave herself. Father, of course, said blankly she married for money, or at best because she *had* to, seeing that old Mr. Letterby was up to his ears in debt and Matho had a mortgage on his estate. But Father always disliked her. He loathed her at the end; and that prevented him from seeing that, according to his theory, she was nobly sacrificing herself: wanting Howard, taking Matho for her father's sake. Personally," my sister added with energy, " I don't see it in that way and never have. I don't see Rose in that way. Nor do you, David, if the truth be told." As I did not reply, she added: " Rose wouldn't have sacrificed herself on her father's or on anyone's altar."

" That's a hard saying, Ann."

" Hard it may be, but not cruel," my sister answered. " It cuts both ways and cuts down in the end to a saving truth. She didn't marry for money because — well, because she hadn't enough sense, not that kind of sense. She hadn't been brought up to think about

the *sources* of money, any more than we think about
the sources of our water-supply. You just turn on the
tap and the water runs, and if it stops — well, there's
nothing you personally can do about it, you just wander
about and hope that the plumber will turn up some day.
Applied to money, it isn't an attitude that either you
or I or Father or Howard could ever have, but whatever else it may be it isn't mercenary: it's a good deal
less mercenary than ours. . . . People of Rose's aristocratic kind are much more likely, when they are bored,
to run off and try to live with a waster out of paper
bags than they are to search diligently for a marriage
settlement. She didn't take Matho because he was
rich. . . . Or, really," my sister added slowly, " reject
Howard because he was poor. Remember your
journey to Charing Cross, David. And remember the
water picnic."

Still uncertain of what was in her mind, I asked
whether her reading of what I had written was
her first knowledge of my " journey to Charing
Cross ".

" Howard told me — it must have been a couple of
years later, but before our marriage — that he and Rose
had nearly run away together," Ann replied, " but I
didn't know your part in it until now. . . . Don't you
see: she would never have gone so far, you would
never have had to make that journey to Charing Cross
and back, if she had been a mercenary calculator.
From her point of view, Howard was — " and my
sister paused over her smile — " spectacularly romantic
paper bags ! "

" But not a waster ! "

" No, indeed. That was the trouble. That was

why she quarrelled with him in the way she did at the water picnic. It was rebellion."

" Against what ? "

" Intelligence. Intellect."

" But he was amusing, too. She laughed as much as anyone. He wasn't boringly intellectual. He never is."

" No," Ann replied, " he never is. But the fact remains : his mind is a highly-powered machine, and it alarmed her to hear it ticking. He can be amusing and gay and light-hearted, but it's always — how can I say it except as he says it ? — it's always ' part of his brief '. The one thing on earth Howard can never be is — puppyish. You don't notice it ; you can't be either. And if you find yourself with people who are spontaneously puppyish, you love it ; so does Howard, so do I ; but you couldn't conceivably *live* with it. And the converse is equally true. . . . There's no need to look for elaborate reasons of calculation or heroic self-sacrifice. Matho had no high-powered machine inside him, he was unexacting, he didn't have to *teach* himself puppy-games, and quite simply — though now I'm guessing — she was fond of him."

Ann looked at me, waiting for me to speak. Much that she had said was true, but I thought, and still think, that, in believing Rose to have accepted Matho's comfortable inferiority because she herself was inferior, my sister missed the point.

" So," I said, " you would have advised her to marry him ? "

" In the circumstances, yes."

" What do you mean ' in the circumstances ' ? Would you have given the same advice if it had been possible for her to wait ten years ? "

" Ten years ?   Why ten years ? "

" Because, Ann, I saw a — a quality in her that wasn't ' puppyish '. No one else did. But I did — and it was there. It was there ! And she knew I saw it, and discovered it in herself because I discovered it in her. . . . Isn't that also a basis of marriage ? "

" Of love, perhaps," she replied.

" But it was the basis of your own marriage ! You may distrust my vision. You can't be blind to your own. You saw a quality in Howard that no one else saw. He discovered it in himself because you discovered it."

Her fingers tightened on the arms of her chair. " Its name ? " she said calmly.

I could find no word that had not more of religion in it than was to be associated with Howard. In any case, the word which was to account for her husband's relative failure before men could not be easy to choose, and I hesitated long before replying at last : ' " Quietism."

Her face lighted at that, but she put it away as too great a word. " Ah," she exclaimed, " you mean ' Duets '." She looked back happily and silently over the long memories until she consented with the one word : " Yes."

Thinking that she would say no more, I turned back to the table and had taken up my pen again, when she said : " And hers ? "

" Hers ? "

" The quality in Rose that you discovered ? "

As soon as she asked it, I knew that there was no acceptable answer to that question. When I was young and the world also, when the *Iliad* and the

Odyssey were new books to me, it had been easy to say
that a goddess might put on a mortal disguise and her
face be seen through the mask. But it could not be
said now; the bright coin of language had been bitten
so often by sceptical teeth that it no longer rang true.
The question was unanswerable, and my long silence
became a burden.

Then I saw a way in which a part of the answer
might be given to Ann.

" She had the power," I said, " to work my ' deep
magics '."

My sister threw towards me the strangest of glances
— a swift, almost frightened glance of intense curiosity
which steadied into a long compassionate gaze. She
remembered the phrase from our past.

" You say that as if she still had the power."

" Well, dear Ann, you still play duets. . . . Some
people are lucky; they go into the house. And some
remember what they saw through the window. They
are not unfortunate — if they do remember, clearly
and faithfully."

Ann answered quickly. " I shouldn't have interrupted you, my dear. It is you who must write her
epitaph."

I turned to the table again, incapable of writing.
Howard came in from his own book-room, carrying, in a
dispatch-case, the papers on which he had been at work.

" Well," he said, " that's done. Come to the fire,
David. You look isolated over there. I can't have you
working all the twenty-four hours."

Glad of the excuse, I let the pen roll on the desk.

" What does it look like for to-morrow, David? "
Ann asked. " Have a look out."

I drew back a pair of curtains. At first I could see only myself looking in, but I opened the long window, went out into the garden, and came back to the fire, which was dying down.

"Bright starlight, but cooler than it might be," I reported, and, though the clock on the mantelpiece was striking the half-hour after ten, I threw a couple of logs on to the fire. It was pleasant to sit there between them and talk of nothing much and watch the flames draw pink lines round the edges of my fingers. I wanted them to forget the clock and stay up late. Ann, entering into my conspiracy, took out fresh silks, but Howard began to wind his watch. "Well," he said, "one more needle."

Their bedtime came and Howard went ahead to test the bolts. I returned to this table.

From the fireside Ann told me not to work late and said good-night, but as she passed my chair she leaned down, put her cheek against mine and said: "Finish it, David. Even if it takes all night. And then, promise me, never to touch it again."

"I promise."

I thought she was gone, but she came back and, with an odd hesitancy, told me to keep up a good fire. "Yes, bless you," I answered. Then, suddenly, she put her arms round me from behind and used words that had not passed between us since the night of the Seafords' dance. "Perils and dangers," she said, and was gone.

Since then I have written what follows the words "Lord Chancellorship". No epilogue. No epitaph. Just talk. But there it is. The room is empty and everyone is asleep.

FINAL RETROSPECT

When I was young, all lives but mine
Were windows in a house of stone
From which interior light did shine
     On me, outside, alone.

My judgement, spellbound, did not speak:
In awe, I loved to stand and stare,
Through brilliant eye and glowing cheek,
     At spirits moving there.

Now, inside, if I seek again
What Is in that which seems to be,
My own face, mirrored by the pane,
     Stares askingly at me.

But soon, when agelessly I lie
Alone, outside experience,
The mercies that were plain when I
     Was young and had no sense
Shall, at the window of my seeing,
Reveal in each distracted face
The habitation and the being
     Of innocence and grace.